RETURN TO DYATLOV PASS

J.H. MONCRIEFF

SEVERED PRESS
HOBART TASMANIA

RETURN TO DYATLOV PASS

ISBN: 978-1-925711-74-5

Also by J.H. Moncrieff

Monsters in Our Wake

The Bear Who Wouldn't Leave

GhostWriters series:

City of Ghosts

The Girl Who Talks to Ghosts

Temple of Ghosts

In February 1959, nine experienced Russian skiers set off on an expedition in the Ural Mountains. When an expected telegram didn't arrive from group leader Igor Dyatlov on February 12, and there was still no word from the skiers by the twentieth, searchers left on a rescue mission.

Once they reached the campsite on Dead Mountain, they witnessed a scene horrific enough to give them nightmares for the rest of their lives.

Something had panicked Dyatlov and his friends, who fled their tent by slashing it open with knives. Some of the group was in their underwear and socks, while others had bare feet. The temperature was estimated to have been -13°F when they ran into the snow.

A few of the bodies were recovered right away, while others took months to find. All of the Dyatlov group had suffered extreme trauma, and four of the bodies were crushed so badly that doctors compared the extent of their injuries to those sustained from being hit by a car.

Russian authorities eventually ruled that a "compelling natural force" had caused the deaths. To this day, the tragedy remains a mystery. It is known as the Dyatlov Pass incident.

This book is dedicated in memory to the nine skiers who died on what is now known as the Dyatlov Pass: Igor Alekseievich Dyatlov, Yuri Nikolaievich Doroshenko, Lyudmila Alexandrovna Dubinina, Yuri (Georgiy) Alexeyevich Krivonischenko, Alexander Sergeievich Kolevatov, Zinaida Alekseevna Kolmogorova, Rustem Vladimirovich Slobodin, Nicolai Vladimirovich Thibeaux-Brignolles, and Semyon (Alexander) Alekseevich Zolotaryov.

May they rest in peace.

Ural Mountains, Soviet Union

March 1959

The moment before she died, Lyudmila wondered how it had gone so terribly wrong. Concealed within a makeshift snow cave for warmth and protection, she huddled close to Nicolai, though her friend's body had long grown cold and stiff.

"Remember, Mila," he'd counseled her. *"Whatever you do, do not scream. However frightened you get, whatever happens, you must stay quiet. You will be the one to survive, to tell our families what befell us."*

Her tears had frozen on her cheeks long ago. The air was so frigid it would not allow her to grieve properly. Whatever loneliness and pain she felt at losing her last remaining friend, the man who had given up everything to protect her, must stay locked away. When she'd made it safely home, she would mourn him. But not yet. For now, her focus had to be on survival.

Lyudmila had spent most winters exploring these mountains on skis. She was well versed in the symptoms of hypothermia and frostbite. If she didn't find a way to raise her body temperature soon, she wouldn't draw breath much longer. Ignoring the tingling in her weary arms, she pushed herself away from Nicolai, crawling on her stomach through the snow to the crumpled heap that was Alexander. Of the little group in the cave, Alexander had been the first to die. She averted her eyes from his frozen face as she undid the laces on his boots and tugged. The boots were too big for her, but they were warmer than her own. With the wool socks she'd collected from Semyon, she could make them fit.

She forced several more socks and a boot onto her stiffening foot, flexing her toes while she bit on her lip to keep from crying out. The burning in her extremities, however torturous, was welcome. It meant her feet weren't frostbitten—yet.

A *crack* from the surrounding forest startled her, making her pause with her hands on Alexander's second boot. Another *crack*, followed by a series of rustles and the pattering of cedar branches falling on snow. Lyudmila whimpered before clapping both hands over her mouth, pressing hard enough that her front teeth broke through the skin on her upper lip, flooding her mouth with the metallic tang of her own blood.

"No," she moaned under her breath. "No." She looked at Nicolai, who lay on the other side of their shelter. He was so far away, too far for her to make it in time. She should never have left him. When the others had occasionally mocked her, dismissing her as the youngest in the group, only he had believed in her. He'd called her brave. Though her corneas felt glazed with ice, Lyudmila's eyes welled with tears once more. She dared not let them fall. Her tormentors were attuned to the slightest sound, like foxes poised to hear their dinner scurrying under the snow. She would not scurry, but she would slide back to Nicolai's side. Even in death, he would protect her.

Ignoring her shrieking nerve endings, Lyudmila began the slow, agonizing crawl to her friend. She was a dozen feet away when she heard the worst sound of all, the one they'd come to dread more than any other.

The sound of meat being torn from bone.

Biting her lip again, she focused on Nicky to keep from screaming. Her upper thighs, strong from years of skiing, propelled her forward along the snowpack. *Swish, swish. Swish, swish.* She timed her movements to match the horrible chewing, careful that the slightest rustle of her snow pants was concealed beneath the other sound, but she'd forgotten.

Forgotten the siren call of fresh blood.

In spite of the frigid temperatures, sweat beaded her forehead and trickled down her nose from her efforts. *Swish, swish. Swish, swish.* Dearest Nicky. Soon he would be close enough to touch. The last remaining warmth from his body would renew her courage. At his side, she would survive this night, and in the morning, with his good coat protecting her from the elements, she would attempt to make her way down the mountain to safety.

Lyudmila was inches away from Nicolai's body when a flash of white broke through the snow in front of her, seizing her friend's skull and popping it like an overripe grape. As the deep crimson of Nicky's blood painted their sanctuary the color of death, she forgot her last promise to him.

She screamed.

She was still screaming when her tongue was torn out, along with the inside of her mouth.

~ CHAPTER ONE ~

Nat longed for the days when trolls were grotesque creatures who lurked under bridges in Norway. Sadly, trolls lurked in one's inbox now, and there was no getting rid of them until they grew bored and moved on. If she could have sent this particular one to the fjords, she would have in a heartbeat.

"Another death threat?"

"Huh?" Nat tore her attention away from her screen long enough to see Andrew grin at her.

"I've worked with you long enough to know that sigh. What was it this time? Death threat? Sexual harassment? Some good old-fashioned stalking?"

"None of the above. Good old-fashioned baiting."

As the host of *Nat's Mysterious World,* the US's most popular podcast dealing with the supernatural and unsolved mysteries, Nat was used to hearing from whackos. But this guy was different. He'd been writing her for the past three weeks, the tone of his emails just shy of incendiary. Worst of all, he'd been hitting her where it hurt. She should delete his messages unread and block him before he stole another minute of her precious time, but he was like a car accident she couldn't look away from.

This troll wasn't like other trolls. The guy knew his stuff.

"Cliff again?"

"Yeah," she admitted, bracing herself for a lecture. The road was a well-traveled one.

"I don't understand why you haven't blocked him yet. Why are you wasting your time on that asshole?"

"I should; you're right." Nat ran her fingers through her platinum crop, tugging at the roots. No matter what, she couldn't take her bad mood out on Andrew, who was her producer, as well as the closest thing she had to a friend. "I guess I haven't been willing to give him the satisfaction. I'm sure that's exactly what he wants, proof that he's gotten to me."

"But he *has* gotten to you. Pretending he hasn't is costing you more than giving in. Once he's blocked, it's over. You'll move on and forget you ever heard from him."

If only it were that easy. "He'll probably set up another account."

"Those creeps never do. You know that. They have their fun, and once it's over, they move on and torment someone else."

"You really don't think he has a point?" Nat studied Andrew's face, fancying she'd be able to tell if he lied to her. Though he'd recently celebrated his thirtieth birthday, her producer could pass for a high school kid, and thankfully, he still had the energy of one.

"No," he said, his bottle-green eyes meeting hers without flinching. "I really don't. I think he's full of shit, and the fact this jerk is getting to you pisses me off."

"Thanks." To humor him, she deleted the email, but it didn't matter. Cliff's words would run through her mind for at least the next hour or three, torturing her. "But maybe he's right. Maybe this show has become all talk. It's been a long while since I've done anything noteworthy."

"And what's he done, besides jerk off and spew hatred from behind his computer? Probably lives in his mom's basement, eating Cheetos and swigging Mountain Dew."

A ghost of a smile played over her lips. That was exactly how she pictured Cliff. But Cheetos or no Cheetos, it didn't mean the guy was wrong. In years past, no adventure had been too dangerous or too difficult. She'd braved Poveglia, otherwise known as the most haunted island in the world. She'd spent the night in the Winchester Mystery House, explored the bowels of the *Queen Mary* with only a flashlight, and puked her guts out in Romania's *Hoia Baciu*.

Lately, though, she'd become complacent. Sure, she'd go on the odd ghost tour or hunt for Bigfoot in a national park, but there hadn't been anything remotely risky in far too long. Troll or no troll, Cliff was right. She talked the talk without walking the walk. She'd lost her authenticity, the very thing that had made her cast popular in the first place.

"Look, he's a freak. He's obsessed. You need to let it go. You don't have time to worry about the Cliffs of the world and their deranged opinions."

It was true; she didn't. But still...

"It would be one hell of a challenge though, wouldn't it? That story has always bugged me. Did you know it's been almost sixty years, and they still have no idea what happened to those people?"

Andrew rolled his eyes. "And they never will. It's a loser, Nat. Not to mention suicide."

She bristled, as he'd no doubt expected. In his own way, Andrew was pretty damn good at baiting her too. "You forget I'm Canadian. I'm not soft like you."

"Yeah, yeah. Spare me your stories of growing up in an igloo and getting to school on a dogsled. You were raised in Vancouver, which is hardly the Russian mountains."

"Vancouver is where I went to college, not where I was raised. Shows how little you know. We may not have had igloos in my hometown, but the Iditarod champion lived just down the block."

"Whatever. Is that really how you want to spend your vacation, freezing your ass off on some godforsaken Russian mountain, attempting to solve a mystery that's almost six decades old?"

"You have to admit, it sounds like fun, doesn't it?" Cliff's latest taunt-fest forgotten, her mind was already packing. "Gets the blood racing again."

"Schlepping around on a suicide mission is the opposite of fun. Not to mention it's been done—if you'll forgive the expression—to death."

Calling Nat unoriginal was almost as bad as calling her a coward. "By whom? When?"

"Come on, Nat. Everyone and their uncle's BuzzFeed has written about the Dyatlov Pass incident. It's hardly groundbreaking. If you're going to risk your life, at least find some nice possessed girl no one else has discovered yet."

She snorted, hoping to convey an appropriate amount of disdain. "Those listicles? They don't come close to doing it justice. All they do is recycle the same Wikipedia content and slap a new byline on it. If I were to do this, I'd do it right. Get a team together and investigate what really happened out there. Who knows, maybe we'd come up with some answers. Or at least an interesting theory."

"Gee, that's never been done. No one's ever made a *movie* about it."

"That was fiction, Andrew. And I'm hardly a wet-behind-the-ears film student with delusions of grandeur."

"No, you're an experienced journalist. Which is why I'm shocked you're even considering this. What makes you think the Russian government would cooperate? Trust me, it's a waste of time. You're letting this guy bait you into an early grave."

"Have you no mystery in your soul? Doesn't it intrigue you, even a little?" The more he argued against it, the more excited she got. All her best ideas had begun with people insisting she was insane. It wasn't like wandering a deserted island infested with the bubonic plague had been the wisest course of action, but people loved that shit. Her ratings had skyrocketed, and the sponsors had followed. "Let me put it this way— would a nice big raise intrigue you?"

The corner of Andrew's mouth twitched. Just for a second, but it was enough. "Fine," he said. "I'll call the Russian embassy this afternoon."

"You're awesome."

"And you're insane."

"Thanks." Slipping on her earphones, she hummed along to the music.

5

It had been too long since someone had called her that. And damn, it felt good.

~ CHAPTER TWO ~

Her cell woke her in the middle of the night, which for Nat was more like three in the morning. Startled from a nightmare where the Russians had rejected her passport and thrown her in the gulag, she groped for the phone, disoriented.

"Andrew?"

She'd almost gotten used to her producer calling her at all hours. Once he'd realized she wasn't going to change her mind about Dyatlov, he'd jumped into preparations wholeheartedly, and part of that was assembling the best team on the planet. That meant Canadians. Nat didn't care how many champion rock climbers resided in California—she wanted people who understood cold, who had experience surviving extreme temperatures. It had taken Andrew a while to succumb to her logic (and to see that it *was* logic, not some twisted form of patriotism for the old country) but once he did, he'd embraced it with a vengeance. He'd managed to convince a young Inuit couple to come along for the ride. Anubha and her husband Joe followed the traditional ways, and Anubha was a skilled tracker. Her knowledge of arctic wildlife would serve the team well. While Nat had no desire to turn her investigation into a survival show, it was wise not to depend entirely on their supplies.

So far, Andrew had soared over every hurdle she'd put in front of him. Except one. Nat wanted a Mansi on the team. She didn't believe that bullshit about the native tribe being unwilling to set foot on Dead Mountain. Not for a second. Everyone had a price.

This had to be her producer phoning in triumph, telling her he'd achieved every condition she'd set.

"Andrew, you're a genius. How on earth did you find one?"

"I'm happy to see you're taking my advice."

Nat stiffened. The voice, rough as a cheese grater over gravel, was not her producer's. "Who is this?"

"You know who it is. What you should be asking is why it took me so long to call."

"Cliff."

"Bingo."

She clutched the sheets tighter, bringing them closer around her body. "How did you get this number?" Her cell was unlisted, private. Very few people had access to it, and that was the way she liked it. She certainly didn't share it with her audience.

"You're not the only one who can do research."

"Call me again and I'll report you," she said, her voice strong and unwavering, belying how spooked she was.

"For making a phone call? What's my crime?" As rough as his voice was, it was also smooth like a radio announcer's. Nat thought she'd heard it somewhere before. Maybe if she kept him on the line, she'd remember where.

"Stalking."

He laughed. "I'm hardly *stalking* you, Ms. McPherson. If I were, I'd be outside your bedroom window right now." Waiting a beat, long enough for her arms to break out in goose bumps, he said, "Don't worry; I'm not."

She swallowed around the lump that had formed in her throat. "Email and phone calls count as stalking too."

"I'm not a stalker. I'm a fan. Do you have so few you can't recognize them?"

"I wouldn't call you a fan, Cliff." Remembering some of his harshest criticisms, her face flushed. "You're a troll. A spiteful, petty troll with too much time on his hands."

"Now, is that any way to talk to the *fan* who gave you the best idea of your career?"

"You hardly gave me the idea. I've been interested in the Dyatlov Pass incident for years."

"Is that a fact? Why didn't you do something about it before, then? Why did you wait for me to goad you?"

His audacity brought her to the brink of trembling rage. Who did this asshole think he was? Did he actually believe he had power over her? Andrew was right—this guy was a creep, and nothing more. "No one goaded me into this expedition. Do you have any clue about the amount of preparation, not to mention money, something like this takes? I would never go to this kind of trouble because someone double-dog dared me. I'm not twelve years old."

He laughed again. "Having trouble sharing the credit? That's fine. I understand."

"Don't call me again, Cliff."

"Hang up if you want. I just thought you might want to speak with someone intimately connected with the case."

"And who would that be?" She was exhausted and irritated beyond belief, but her innate curiosity always got the better of her. She was like a cat that way.

"Me."

"Right. *You* are connected to the Dyatlov case."

"From the hostility in your tone, it's obvious you don't believe me, but I assure you I am. Why else would I be so insistent? I have a personal stake in this."

8

This guy was unbelievable. Not only a stalker, but mentally unstable as well. Fantastic. "Forgive me for saying so, Cliff, but you don't sound Russian."

"After the death of my great-aunt, my family was so traumatized they emigrated to America. I grew up on US soil, just as you did."

So he didn't know she was Canadian, an immigrant herself. At least there were limitations to his stalking prowess. "Oh yeah? And who was your aunt?"

"Lyudmila Dubinina."

Nat shivered. It was a lot colder in her room all of a sudden. "You're Lyudmila's great-nephew?"

"That I am."

"I find that incredibly difficult to believe." But wasn't a part of her already believing it?

"What reason would I have to lie? I told you, I have a stake in this."

She was impressed in spite of herself. Even with the never-ending fascination surrounding the case, few people could name any of the skiers beyond Igor Dyatlov, and many didn't know his first name. Then again, if pretending to be Lyudmila's nephew were Cliff's shtick, he would have done his research.

"If that's true, why didn't you say so? Why the nasty emails? Why not introduce yourself and say you wanted me to look into your great-aunt's death, like a normal person would?"

"Because you needed a push. Over the years, you've grown lazy, apathetic. If I'd asked for your help, you would have made a few phone calls, maybe, talked about it on your cast, but you would never have gone to the pass. Forgive my crudeness, Ms. McPherson, but someone needed to light a fire under your ass."

"If Lyudmila were really your aunt, I'm sure she wouldn't approve of your harassing a woman."

"My aunt was a strong woman. She would have understood that sometimes the end justifies the means."

"Assuming I believe you, and I'm not saying I do, what do you think happened to her?"

"That's an easy question to answer. She was murdered before I was born."

"Murdered. You don't believe the avalanche theory, I take it."

Cliff chuckled. "No, I don't. I also don't believe that ridiculous infrasound theory or paradoxical undressing, either."

"What *do* you believe?"

"As I've said, my aunt was an incredibly strong woman. She was also an experienced skier. She'd been exploring and camping on those mountains since she was a girl. There's no way she would have set up camp in the path of an avalanche, Ms. McPherson. This was murder."

Of the nine dead hikers, Nat had always felt the closest connection to Lyudmila, probably because the woman had suffered the most. She'd also been the youngest member of the group, only twenty-one years old.

While the rest of the skiers' bodies had been discovered in February, the same month they went missing, poor Lyudmila and her three hapless friends had to wait until May, when searchers finally found their remains buried under twelve feet of snow.

Whoever had found her must have been traumatized for life. Lyudmila's eyes, part of her lips, and a piece of her skull were missing, her nose was broken and flattened, and she had severe head injuries. Four of her ribs were broken on her right side and seven on the left side. Her chest was fractured. She'd suffered a massive hemorrhage in her heart's right atrium, and her left thigh was badly bruised. The doctor who'd examined her body said an unknown compelling force had caused Lyudmila's trauma, explaining that the power required for such damage was akin to a car hitting her.

But that was hardly the worst of it.

Her tongue and the muscles from inside her mouth were missing. The amount of blood in her stomach suggested the tissue had been removed while she was still alive.

"My aunt had defensive wounds on her hands. Before she died, she fought for her life. This wasn't something that happened to her after death. She was conscious when something ripped her tongue out and tortured her. She was *aware*."

Wincing at the terrible image of what the young woman must have suffered, Nat mentioned the same quandary Andrew had voiced for months. "This happened almost sixty years ago. What do you expect me to find?"

"There's something on that mountain. Something that killed my aunt and her friends, and it isn't human. The doctor who examined the bodies admitted no human has the strength to kill this way."

That much was true. She'd read detailed translations of the original autopsy reports. A high level of radiation had been found on some of the bodies. There were so many things that were puzzling about this case.

"What makes you think whatever it is will still be there?"

"I can't explain why I feel the way I do. Call it a hunch, call it intuition, call it my aunt's spirit guiding me from beyond the grave. But I believe, without a doubt, that you are the one to find out what happened to her. Don't let me down."

Before she could thank him for the vote of confidence, he hung up, leaving her with dead air and the nightmarish vision of a woman fighting for her life.

~ CHAPTER THREE ~

I've made a mistake.

The thought had first nibbled at the corners of Nat's conviction that morning, when she'd met "her" Mansi, a slight man with short, wavy hair and a heavily lined face. Vasily spoke strongly accented English that required no translator.

"You're certain you don't have any problem taking us up there?" she'd asked once introduced, hoping for a pithy sound bite about the horrors of *Kholat Syakhl*, the infamous Dead Mountain.

The man regarded her with dark eyes that were surprisingly cold. "Prefer not to, but times, they are difficult. Many of my people are starving. Others are leaving the community. I will do what must be done."

It sounded ominous but Nat soldiered on, determined not to let the Mansi discourage her. "When should we meet you tomorrow?"

Vasily looked at each member of her group before responding. Anubha, the startlingly beautiful Inuit tracker. Her husband Joe, who appeared to be more than a little rough around the edges. The appropriately named Igor, a blond Russian ski instructor who smiled and nodded so frequently Nat questioned how much he understood. Lana, a Canadian survival expert who'd once been an Olympic alpine skier. Steven, an amateur mountaineer from California. And finally, herself and Andrew.

Andrew, a California boy through and through, shivered in his brand new parka, stamping his feet to warm them. They'd been outside for less than ten minutes. For the hundredth time, Nat considered leaving him behind at their hotel in Vizhai, but her producer had always been a part of these adventures. It wouldn't be the same without him, like undertaking a hike with a missing limb.

Originally, the plan had been to assemble a group of nine who would mirror the characteristics and demographics of Dyatlov's friends, but that soon proved to be impossible, as well as dangerous. Choosing someone because they were young, blonde, and Russian rather than adept at hiking and surviving was pure madness, as much as it would have made for a great show.

"They are ready, your group? They have trained? The pass is Category III. It is difficult terrain. Only the very experienced should go."

Nat met Andrew's eyes, sympathizing with the panic she saw there. Out of their group of seven, the producer was the least prepared, closely followed by her. Unlike the others, they were not elite athletes or survival experts. They *had* trained until their muscles had ached and each new pain had become indistinguishable from the last, but still—climbing mountains in California was hardly in the same category as what they'd experience tomorrow. Nat's naturally slim frame had turned wiry and nearly gaunt with all the unaccustomed exercise, which wouldn't stand her well if she ended up stranded on the pass somewhere. She resolved to stick close to Anubha. Or perhaps Vasily was her better bet, since he was the one with the gun.

"Yes, we have." She lifted her chin slightly at the expression of doubt that flitted across the Mansi's face. What she didn't have in athletic prowess, she more than made up for in stubbornness. She'd carry Andrew to the pass on her back if need be.

"Do your people really believe the mountain is cursed?" Lana asked.

Vasily's response was a look so withering the Olympian visibly shrank inside her Canada Goose parka. "My 'people' live in the real world. We do not believe in fairy stories. Kholat Syakhl is a bad place, but not because of any curse."

"What do you mean? What makes it bad?" Nat jumped in, feeling she should rescue her fellow Canadian, whose cheeks were flushed and not by the cold.

He shrugged. "The weather. The terrain. The wildlife. A lot of risk for little return."

"Wildlife? I thought you called it Dead Mountain because there was no game up there?" Steven's question had an edge to it, just enough of a challenge that Nat wondered if they were going to have a problem with the mountaineer. She wished they'd had more time to acclimate as a group and learn each other's weaknesses and strengths before they braved the hike. But time, as they say, was money.

"Perhaps the bears and wolves did not get the memo," Vasily replied. Anubha chuckled under her breath.

Bears and wolves. Some people speculated that a wild animal had caused Lyudmila's facial trauma. But what animal removes its victim's tongue and eyes, leaving the rest of the face intact? Nat shivered. The Mansi certainly hadn't been hired for his winning personality.

Igor spoke to Vasily in Russian and both men laughed. Maybe she did need a translator after all. Were they laughing at her? It wasn't a comforting thought.

"We should leave at dawn if we're going to make the first camp before it gets dark," Igor said, flashing his perfect teeth at her. "It will be a very long day. We need much rest."

"That seems like a good idea. Seven, then?" Andrew asked, and Nat didn't miss the amused look that passed between Igor and Vasily.

"Five," Vasily said, staring down her producer as if daring him to argue. Andrew, who often called it a night at five in the morning, swallowed hard.

"I suggest we have dinner and then turn in. We've arranged for a feast in a traditional restaurant nearby." Nat infused as much cheer into her words as she could, in spite of the feelings of trepidation that crept over her. Had they done the wrong thing, choosing the team based on skill rather than personality? Everyone was so different, their only common ground a love of the outdoors. Though perhaps love wasn't the right word for it, especially in Vasily's case.

As though he'd read her mind, Vasily slung his pack over his shoulder. "I prefer to have a simple meal in my room. I will see you here at five tomorrow." He left without waiting for a reply.

"Anyone else?" Nat asked, mentally crossing her fingers. She was concerned Igor would follow suit, but the ski instructor stayed where he was. She was fairly certain it was the promise of an extravagant meal that kept him rooted to the spot rather than their company. "All right, let's go. Five o'clock is going to come early."

To their credit, no one groaned. As the group fell in line, Lana chatted with Anubha and her husband while Igor and Steven shared war stories of mountain life. Still, the Mansi's attitude clung to Nat like a shroud, and the blast of frigid air that greeted them as they left the hotel certainly didn't help. As much as she talked tough about how hardy Canadians were, that was all it was—talk. There was a reason she'd relocated to California.

"Vasily's sure a charmer, isn't he?" Andrew kept his voice low so it wouldn't carry to the rest of the group.

"Thankfully, we didn't hire him for his charm. If he gets us to Dyatlov Pass and back in one piece, that's good enough for me."

"If?" Her producer had a gift for picking up on the slightest nuance. "Are you having doubts?"

Nat pulled her muffler higher on her cheeks, eyes tearing in the bitter wind. "We trained for six months, Andrew. Dyatlov's group did this sort of thing for most of their lives and look what happened to them. Having doubts means I'm of sound mental health. It would be insane not to have doubts."

"I guess so. Whatever happened to them—you don't really think it's still out there, do you?"

"I think our biggest challenges are going to be the weather, exertion, and our own paranoia. Whatever killed Igor and his friends, there's no way it's still out there sixty years later."

She hoped she sounded more confident than she felt. The truth was, she had no idea what had happened to the Dyatlov group. What had terrified nine experienced outdoorsmen so much they cut open their tent and ran into the cold in their underwear? Why had Lyudmila's group survived so much longer and sustained such terrible and strange injuries? Where did the radiation on the bodies come from, and why were the tops of the trees near some of them burned? Something had terrified the skiers, and judging by what had befallen them, rightly so. But what? There were a million theories, all of them ultimately unsatisfying.

"Fuck, it's freezing. Couldn't you have decided to solve the mystery of the Bermuda Triangle instead?"

Linking arms with Andrew, Nat smiled, huddling closer to her producer for warmth. "Maybe that should be our reward for surviving this."

If you survive it.

That nasty voice in her head again, the one that kept insisting she'd made a mistake. But of course they'd survive it. Why wouldn't they? They had the best team, the most sophisticated equipment. Whatever had happened to Lyudmila and her friends back in the 1950s had to have had a rational explanation. Her job was to find it, not to die trying.

"Vasily gives me the creeps," Andrew said.

"He's not the most amiable fellow, is he? But consider things from his point of view. His way of life is dying out, and to feed his family, he has to drag a group of ill-prepared tourists up one of the region's most dangerous mountains. If he's a little grumpy, can't say I blame him."

"Ill-prepared tourists? I take offense to that."

"You know what I mean. Just looking at it from his perspective. He has no idea how amazing our team is."

"That's better."

As they followed the rest of the group to the restaurant, Nat tried to pinpoint what was bothering her. Was it Vasily's doom-and-gloom demeanor? The eeriness of following in the footsteps of nine people who'd died horrible, unexplained deaths? Or something more?

"We're going to be okay, right?"

The concern in Andrew's voice echoed her own thoughts. She squeezed his arm. "Of course we're going to be okay. We're going to be sitting in the sun with margaritas, laughing about this, before you know it."

"I hope you're right."

Me too.

* * *

The Russians who welcomed them to dinner were friendly and cheerful, passing around generous glasses of homemade vodka as soon as their group arrived. Lana looked doubtfully at her share as it slid down the worn wooden table into her hand.

"I'm not sure we should be drinking. We're going to need to be on top of our game tomorrow."

"A little vodka never hurt anyone," Igor said, downing his shot with a hearty *"Na zdorovie!"* He grinned, clinking his empty glass against hers before grabbing another. "It warms the blood. Try it."

Nat held her breath as she waited for the Olympian's response. She wasn't sure about Russia, but in many countries, refusing a drink was considered an insult.

"I guess one wouldn't hurt." With a tentative smile, Lana took a small sip that immediately set off a coughing fit. She clutched her chest, her eyes streaming. "Wow, that's strong."

Everyone laughed as Igor pounded her on the back. "You see? It's good stuff. Puts hair on your chest."

"Well now, that's *exactly* what I need." Wiping her eyes, Lana sat beside the Russian, leaving the rest of her glass untouched, but the ice had been broken. Nat could breathe again. From this brief exchange, it appeared their group was going to get along fine.

She was surprised when Steven took the chair next to hers. He was the one she knew the least about. He'd been a last-minute addition, but Andrew had said the mountaineer's credentials were so extraordinary he couldn't refuse. Nat suspected the man's dark good looks and startlingly blue eyes hadn't hurt.

Their hosts refilled the glasses and passed stoneware bowls of soup down the table, along with thick slices of dark rye bread. Nat leaned over the bowl so the steam could caress her face, thawing her still-frozen nose. The soup was a lovely, if surprisingly vivid, shade of magenta. *Borscht.*

"Nervous about tomorrow?"

Steven watched her with an intensity she found unnerving, as if those turquoise eyes of his could see right through her. She considered lying, but decided on a half-truth. "A little. You?"

"Nah. I survived Everest. What these guys call a Category III is nothing." He buttered his slice of bread, but his attention remained focused on her. It was everything she could do to keep from squirming. Beautiful men had always made her uncomfortable. Why on earth had she left a gay man in charge of choosing the team?

"You climbed Everest? What was that like?" She'd never met anyone who'd braved the world's highest mountain before. Though she didn't have similar aspirations, people who did fascinated her. There was so much risk, both personally and financially. Climbers had to pay at least thirty-five thousand dollars just to have a go at it, with no guarantee they'd ever make it to the top. And even if the weather cooperated enough to make an attempt at the summit, the mountain was littered with the bodies of those who had failed.

"Phenomenal. It's one of the greatest experiences the world has to offer. I highly recommend it."

His unwavering gaze made her uneasy. Nat concentrated on her soup, focusing on spooning the warm beet-and-beef concoction into her mouth. Spiked with a hint of fresh dill, it managed to be hearty and refreshing at the same time. "Oh, I'm not at that level. I probably wouldn't make it to Base Camp."

Never mind not being able to afford it. Her podcast did well, but not well enough she could throw away thirty-five grand on a single experience, and a gamble at that.

"Don't sell yourself short. I bet you can do anything you set your mind to."

Nat looked up, startled at the compliment. "Thank you. That's a nice thing to say, especially considering you hardly know me."

"How's it going?" Andrew whispered on her other side, probably jealous Steven had chosen to sit beside her. Her producer had already taken to calling the mountaineer "McDreamy" behind his back. She bumped his leg under the table, their universal signal for *Not now*.

"Oh, I know you better than you think. I've listened to every episode of *Nat's Mysterious World*."

"You have?" She knew she had loyal listeners, but every episode? A weekly cast for five years added up to...well, a lot of episodes.

"Yes, I have." Was that a glimmer of amusement in his eyes? "Didn't your producer tell you I'm a fan? I think that's what convinced him to let me come."

"He must have forgotten to mention it." She gave Andrew a kick under the table, more for pure enjoyment than retribution.

Huge platters of food arrived and Igor stood to address the group. He was beaming, clearly in his element. Nat was warming to him. Every team needed a life of the party.

"You are in for a treat, my good friends. These are *blini*, otherwise known as Russian pancakes. They are better than what you are used to in the West, yah? Made of buckwheat." He spoke to their hosts in his native language before continuing. "Elena says there is smoked salmon, homemade sour cream, and caviar. If you don't like the fish, try the mushrooms. Yours to enjoy. *Priyatnogo appetita!*"

Another platter, this time of chicken, lamb, and beef skewers, needed no explanation, nor did the Russian potato salad. Nat's stomach rumbled as she piled her plate high, forgetting to worry about her dinner companion for a moment.

"How did you get interested in this stuff?"

"Umph?" Nat mumbled around a mouthful of smoked salmon and buckwheat. *Mmm, bliss.* She normally wasn't a fan of sour cream, but this homemade version bore no resemblance to the tasteless stuff found in grocery stores.

Steven gave her a patient smile. His plate showed a lot more moderation than hers. "I asked how you got interested in this."

"What, food?" Because food was all she cared about right now. Perhaps the others could brave Kholat Syakhl while she stayed here with the borscht and blini.

"No, the weird stuff. Monsters, UFOs, ghosts. The paranormal, I guess you'd call it."

"Actually, it's more unsolved mysteries that intrigue me. I like to keep an open mind. The rest of it comes with the territory, I guess." Nat wondered why she had to explain this if Steven was such a fan of her show. If he'd listened to every episode, wouldn't he know this already? "When someone has had something incredible happen to them, something not a lot of people would believe or even understand, they naturally gravitate to a receptive audience. I try my best to be that audience."

"But why? What made you interested to begin with? Did something happen to you?"

Nat stifled a sigh. This was what it was about, this dinner—getting to know each other, becoming a team. But she wished Steven would give it a rest and eat his meal for a few minutes. His constant focus on her was making her self-conscious. Still, it would be rude to ignore him.

"Not really. That is, nothing major. I've definitely been in places that have a *feel* about them, something that gives you goosebumps and sets your teeth on edge, but beyond that and the odd unexplained sound, I haven't had a paranormal experience myself."

"Unexplained sound?"

"Yeah. You know, doors closing by themselves. Rustling, bumps in the night with no explanation. Pretty standard ghost tour stuff."

"But you'd like to experience more."

It was a statement, not a question, but from the way Steven stared at her, Nat knew he expected an answer. She thought for a moment, taking the opportunity for another bite of blini, this time with mushrooms. *Mmm.* Who knew Russian food was so tasty? She'd expected a lot of cabbage and potatoes, and not much else.

"Enjoy it while you can," Andrew muttered, as if reading her mind. "Starting tomorrow, it's dehydrated spaghetti and astronaut ice cream."

Ick. She wasn't looking forward to the food at camp. Never mind the terrain—the cuisine, or lack thereof, would be the thing to survive.

"You'd be surprised. A lot of the food in those foil packets is actually really good," Lana said. "Especially after a long day on the trail. You'll think it's the best meal you've ever had in your life."

"And Joe and I will supplement our meals with fresh meat," Anubha said. "I've brought my crossbow. We're ready to do some serious hunting."

"Fresh meat roasted over a campfire. There is nothing better," Igor said, and everyone murmured in agreement. Everyone except Steven. What was wrong with this guy? Was he one of those strange "eat to live" people?

"Sounds like we'll be living like royalty up there," Nat chimed in, eager to bring the one-on-one with her dining companion to an end. Normally she was more than happy to answer questions about the cast, but there was something about Steven's scrutiny that made her long for a shower.

"We'll be suffering enough on the trail. No need to suffer in camp. If we get lucky, Anubha makes a roasted rabbit that will blow your mind," Joe said.

Andrew reached for another kebab. "Sounds good to me."

"I've never eaten rabbit before." Lana wrinkled her nose. "I don't know if I can eat something that's cute and fuzzy."

"What about lamb?" Igor gestured at the half-eaten skewer on her plate. "It's cute and fuzzy."

"That's lamb? I thought it was beef!"

Everyone laughed at Lana's exaggerated expression of horror. Again, everyone but Steven. Lana had clearly taken on the role of comedic relief in their group, whether intentionally or not. From what Andrew had told her, the blonde was actually super sharp. Nat couldn't help wondering if the dimwitted Marilyn Monroe persona was an act.

"So you think only cute animals should be allowed to live? You do not think cows are cute?"

Uh oh. Nat suspected Igor was just goading Lana, but this conversation could quickly take a dark turn. Joe stepped in before she could.

"Let's move on. We're all friends here, right? No one's going to be forced to eat anything. There's no pressure. Anubha and I will catch what we can, and we'll be happy to share it with whoever wants it. But we won't think badly of you if you don't."

Andrew nudged her arm. She knew what he was thinking. *The diplomat.* There was one in almost every group. Nat was glad theirs was Joe. Before she could pat herself on the back too much, though, Steven spoke to the group for the first time that evening.

"That's a bit presumptuous, don't you think?"

Lana's rosebud mouth fell open. Even Igor was speechless. Only Joe appeared unfazed by the mountaineer's rudeness. "I'm sorry…what's a bit presumptuous?"

"Saying we're all friends. The truth is, we don't know each other. And up on that mountain, things are going to get very real very fast. It'll be every man and woman for themselves. I've seen it before."

"That's not a positive attitude," Lana said. "Maybe we don't know each other well yet, but we will by the end of the week. And I hope we'll be friends." She smiled around the table. Anubha smiled back.

"I'm not here to be positive. I'm here to survive. I suggest that be your focus as well, if you want to last until the end of the week."

Nat inched farther away from Steven, until her thigh was pressed against Andrew's. *Ugh.* Her first impression had been right. This guy was a jerk.

"I know you're very experienced, but with all due respect, this isn't Everest," she said. "Our survival isn't in question."

"Are you deluded? You're all acting like this is some kind of celebration, stuffing your faces and swilling the moonshine. Have you forgotten what we're here to do? Have you forgotten what happened to those people?"

"Of course we haven't forgotten. That's why we're here," Anubha said.

"I'm sorry, but maybe some of us are grateful to be given this chance, and to be here in Russia." Lana frowned. "I, for one, think it's a wonderful opportunity, and I'm glad to be a part of it. If you can't appreciate it, why are you here?"

Good question, Nat thought. *Why are you here? A Category III trail obviously poses no challenge for you, so why do it?*

"Appreciate it? *Appreciate* it? Am I the only one here who's not suicidal? Why would I appreciate risking my own life?"

"No offense, Steven, but we're hardly risking our lives. It will be challenging, yah, but you've survived worse and are here to tell about it. What are you afraid of?" Igor asked.

"What am I afraid of? I'm afraid of the same thing that killed Dyatlov and his people. And if you're not..." Steven glared at each member of their group in turn. When his ice-blue eyes settled on her, Nat found it impossible to look away. "And if you're not, you've got a death wish."

~ CHAPTER FOUR ~

The chill in the air was nothing compared to the coldness within their group. *Shit.* Nat had hoped a good night's sleep would restore some of the cheerful optimism that had existed before Steven's outburst, but it was soon clear it hadn't.

She hadn't seen so many unhappy faces since the last election. Only Igor looked to be in decent spirits, but even he gave the mountaineer a wide berth, as though whatever troubled Steven were contagious. And Steven *was* troubled—of that, she had no doubt. Nat didn't think he was intentionally trying to be a temperamental douchebag.

The man was scared.

"Andrew." Bumping him with her elbow, she nodded to where Steven stood apart from the group. At least her producer would keep McDreamy company, even if the job wouldn't be nearly as pleasant as he'd originally hoped.

"I know," he whispered. "But neither of us will be able to keep up with him."

He was right. As soon as Vasily was ready, Steven pushed his way to the head of the group beside the Mansi, where they walked together in silence. If it wasn't exactly companionable, at least it wasn't hostile.

"What do you think?"

Nat knew what Andrew meant. *What was Steven's problem?* He'd fought to get on this excursion, so why say all that stuff about not appreciating it? What had motivated him to campaign for a spot on their team? It couldn't just be the podcast. There had to be more.

"I'm not sure," she said. "But I intend to find out. Something's up with that guy."

Part of her thought Steven had a point, however poorly he'd expressed it. They were investigating the fate of nine young people who had been cut down in their prime, after all. The occasion demanded some solemnity. She refused to dance on any graves.

The sky was gray and overcast, matching Nat's mood. She longed for a little sunshine, but knew colder temperatures would come with it. That was yet another advantage they had over the Dyatlov group. It was warmer than it had been when the young Russian skiers had set off on their journey, with no storm in sight.

The trail began at a sharp incline and continued steadily upward. Nat's calf muscles soon began to ache, and she wished she'd taken the time to get a good massage before leaving the States. She consoled herself by noticing that the chatter among her group had died off as everyone concentrated on putting one foot in front of the other. Only

Vasily and Steven, far ahead of the others, didn't seem affected. Anubha and Joe had opted for snowshoes over skis, and even their energetic pace had slowed. Nat hoped no one could hear her wheeze.

She focused on Anubha's cobalt blue parka until her eyes watered. Left, right. Keep pushing forward. Right, left. Breathe (gasp). Left, right. Nat blinked, surprised to see that hot pink had replaced the cobalt blue.

"How are you doing?" Lana's tone was casual, but Nat could see the sympathy in the Olympian's eyes. She felt a temporary rush of resentment.

"Fine." With a Herculean effort, Nat managed not to puff. "And you?"

"Oh, I'm great. I owe you both a lot for getting me back in the wilderness. This is so good for me. I'd really let myself go after the games. Depression, you know."

Nat couldn't imagine the perky woman depressed. She wondered again if this chipper routine was a persona Lana slipped into along with her snowsuit. "Our pleasure."

"You have to understand, this comes as naturally to me as breathing. I've spent most of my life on skis. It would be a completely different story for a recreational skier, even one who's fit. Are you sure you're both okay?"

The way Lana directed her question to Nat and someone over Nat's shoulder indicated that Andrew was still with them. Good. For the last mile or so, she'd been too exhausted to check.

"A...break...would be...nice," Andrew said, sounding more drained than he did after an all-night recording session. What if he (or someone else) had a heart attack out here? Did anyone on the team have more than the most basic first aid skills? It was something she hadn't considered.

"I think it's close to lunch. I'm sure the others are feeling the same way. I'll speak to Vasily." And with that, she was gone, easily gliding past Anubha, Joe, and Igor.

"She...makes it...look...so easy."

"Save your breath. You're probably...going to need it." After slowing down enough to speak to Lana, it took all her strength to resume her former speed. Nat could no longer keep from gasping. Sweat trickled over her nose, coating her lips with salt.

"Attention, everyone."

Exhausted, Nat forced herself to look at the head of the trail, where Steven waved his arms. His voice was clear and confident, easily heard. "We'll stop for lunch at the crest. Shouldn't be longer than another twenty minutes."

Andrew groaned.

"Hang in there, my friend. Just focus on putting one foot in front of the other."

"I…quit."

Nat laughed, even though she couldn't afford to spare the energy. "You can't quit now. How would you get home?"

"Would…find…way."

She risked a peek and was surprised at how miserable her producer looked. His cap and scarf were encrusted with ice, and his eyes watered, leaving red trails on his exposed skin. "If you can't last for twenty minutes, how will you make it back to Vizhai?"

"Fuck…you."

"Stop making me laugh. I can barely breathe as it is."

"Whose…f-fault…is that?"

"Yours." She slipped away before he could catch her, expecting a snowball to connect with her head at any moment. Smiling, she approached the trail with renewed vigor. Andrew always made her feel that way. She often joked he was the love of her life, but it wasn't really a joke. She'd yet to meet a straight man she connected with so well.

The brief exchange had put them farther behind the rest of the group. Nat couldn't see Vasily or Steven anymore, and even Anubha and Joe were a blur. Igor had slowed to wait for them, and when he caught her eye, he waved them on.

"Andy? We have to hurry. We're holding everyone up."

In hindsight, it had been stupid to put the slowest skiers in the back. If the others hadn't noticed they'd fallen behind, what had begun as a lark could have quickly become a life-and-death situation. She'd speak to the group while they ate lunch about changing their formation. Perhaps Igor could bring up the rear.

Rather than seem annoyed when she at last came abreast of him, the Russian grinned, clapping her on the shoulder with such enthusiasm she stumbled. He steadied her by the elbow before she fell. "Don't worry," he said. "It is a tough climb, yah? But we're almost there. You rest soon."

"That'll be good."

"He is okay?" Igor's brow creased in a frown as he regarded Andrew. Nat was dismayed to see how far he had fallen behind.

"He'll be fine. We trained for this, but you know. A gym in California is hardly the Ural Mountains."

"Yah, this mountain, she is something else. But no worry. We wait for your friend, and then we go have lunch. Yes?"

Winded, Nat managed a nod, hoping Igor attributed her flushed cheeks to the cold. Fuck, this was embarrassing. They should have taken a full year, put in a lot more training. What had they been thinking, attempting to keep up with mountaineers and Olympians?

In another minute, Andrew caught up, his face an alarming shade of purple. "Sorry," he gasped.

"No worry, my friend. You okay to go?"

What if Andrew couldn't make it? Nat didn't know what would be worse—figuring out how to get her producer safely back to the village, or being stuck in the middle of nowhere with this contentious group of strangers. Igor, Lana, and the Inuit couple were nice enough, but Steven and Vasily—ugh. She'd never survive a week with them without her best friend.

Thankfully, Andrew managed to regain his wind after a brief rest and they pushed on, Igor setting a slower pace. By the time they reached the crest, the rest of the group was sitting around a roaring fire. Lana, Joe, and Anubha clapped when they arrived. "Hail, hail, the gang's all here. Now we can eat," Joe said. "The good news is, at this part of the trip, we're spoiled for choice. We have beef stew, chili, goulash, spaghetti and meatballs—"

"Ooh! I've never had camp spaghetti and meatballs. Let's try that one." Lana's eyes sparkled as she beamed at the group. Either she was telling the truth about the outdoors rejuvenating her, or she *really* liked spaghetti.

"How could you not have had spaghetti and meatballs? It's a classic," Igor said.

Joe pulled the silver packets from his bag while Anubha gathered snow to melt for cooking water.

"Are you sure that's safe?" Steven asked, and Nat noticed how everyone froze at his question. She wished he'd stay quiet for a while, give the group a chance to forget what a pessimistic asshole he was.

"Am I sure what's safe? Spaghetti?" Joe's voice was calm, but his body language changed, as if he were preparing for a fight, his back rigid and shoulders squared. "Yeah, pretty sure."

"I'm not talking about that processed garbage. I'm talking about what *she's* doing." Steven pointed at Anubha, who glared at the mountaineer.

"My name is Anubha, and there's nothing wrong with this snow. It's perfectly clean."

"What about the things you can't see?"

Andrew groaned, sinking onto a snow-covered log next to Lana, and stretched his hands to the fire. Nat hoped Steven wouldn't take her producer's response personally, but when she glanced at him, he was still staring at Anubha. He hadn't even noticed Andrew.

"What are you talking about?" Joe asked.

"Am I the only one who knows the history? Back when they found the Dyatlov group, their radiation levels were off the charts."

Joe shook his head, black hair flopping to cover one eye. "That was in the '60s. I don't know if you've heard, but the Cold War is over."

"It was 1959, actually, and it doesn't matter. Ever hear of Chernobyl? It won't be safe for another twenty thousand years."

"This is hardly Chernobyl." Andrew couldn't stand people he referred to as "spoilers," those with a knack for spoiling everything they were invited to or included in, and he was already convinced Steven was a spoiler with a vengeance.

"*I think he came on this trip just to ruin everyone's week,*" he'd griped last night after dinner. So much for the startlingly blue eyes and rugged jawline. Physical attributes only went so far with Andy.

"It doesn't have to be. Say the radiation here lasts only a hundred years. That's enough."

Andrew sighed. "You got the Radalert handy, Nat?"

"Yeah, it's right here." She pawed through the front pocket of her backpack, removing the radiation detector. Nat went to give it to her producer, but he shook his head.

"Give it to him," he said, indicating Steven. "He's the one who's so worried about it."

"Look, I'm just trying to be smart about this. I get that I'm a big pain in the ass to everyone, but I'd rather be safe than sorry. I'm sure none of us wants to come down with radiation poisoning."

"You're not a pain in the ass, Steven," Lana said, her voice dripping with sweetness.

Anubha snorted. "Yes, he is. But in this case, he also has a point."

"Thank you." Pushing off his rock, Steven moved closer to her, extending the device close to the snow she was gathering. The machine made a light clicking noise but no beeping as he studied the levels intently. Finally, he straightened. "It looks okay."

"Let's get that snow boiling, babe. We're already behind schedule." Joe cast an uneasy glance at the sky, but Nat couldn't detect anything worrisome. Just the same gray, gray, and more gray.

"I thought you two were going to get us some fresh meat. Wasn't that the deal?"

Nat couldn't get over Steven's audacity. The two Canadians had volunteered to cook lunch for everyone, but the mountaineer was still complaining. Unbelievable.

Anubha ignored him, but her husband appeared to take the man's shot in stride. "Not right now. There's no point in going to the effort when we're only going to be here for an hour."

"Surely it doesn't require that much effort to catch a rabbit or squirrel," Steven said. "Look at this guy." He gestured to Andrew, and my producer shrank further into his parka. "He's running on empty. He needs the protein."

"There's plenty of protein in these packets. They're designed for hikers. That's what they're for." Joe took the pot of snow Anubha handed him and wedged it into the fire.

"They're designed for campers; there's a difference. And they're not real food."

"I'm okay, really. I'm a vegetarian," Andrew said, which was a lie, but Nat hoped it was enough to distract Steven from his tirade. What was wrong with this guy? The worst thing you could do was alienate the people responsible for feeding you.

That got Joe's attention. "Are you able to eat this?"

"Yeah, I can handle that. I'd rather have something that's not as visibly dead as a rabbit or squirrel, if you know what I mean."

"Understandable." Joe shifted the pot so it would get more heat.

"Why is it understandable? It's bullshit. What vegetarian goes on a trip like this? There's no way a vegetarian diet has enough protein and fats to sustain you. Do you know how many calories you're burning by shivering alone?" Steven glared at Andrew. Nat was sure her producer was regretting his impetuousness at this point. Looks were definitely not everything.

"That's actually not true," Lana said. "If you know what you're doing, you can get more than enough protein from a vegetarian diet."

Steven made an odd scoffing noise. "Sure, if he plans to sit here for hours eating nuts and seeds, but we don't have time for that. I can't understand why he came along if he's going to be a weak link."

Summoning more energy than Nat would have suspected possible, Andrew leapt to his feet. "Hey, I've had about enough of you. I'm still the producer, and I can send you back to the States tonight with a nice bill for all your travel expenses."

"Andy..." Nat hoped she could intervene before they reached the point of no return, but perhaps they were already there.

"No, Nat. I know how forgiving you are, but let's face it—it was my mistake to bring this guy on board, and from the first, he's proven to be a real shit. We don't need someone like this on the team."

"I have more right to be on this team than *you* do. What are *you* contributing, besides a lot of lost time and whining?"

27

Nat's mouth fell open. She'd come across some winners in her day, but never someone quite so determined to be unlikeable. "I can't let you talk to my producer that way, Steven. We wouldn't even be here without Andrew. So either you apologize and stop causing trouble with everyone, or you can leave. It's your choice."

"You can't force me to leave." Steven narrowed his eyes.

"Maybe I can't personally, but I'm sure Igor can, if it comes down to that."

Igor raised his hands in the air in a gesture for peace. "Everyone needs to calm down. What are we, children?"

"I agree with Nat. Steven should apologize to Andrew." Lana turned to address the mountaineer. "What you said was mean and uncalled for. No one is the weak link. We all have something to contribute."

Nat fully expected Steven to dig in his heels and really get nasty, but once again he surprised her. "You're right; it was wrong of me to say that. I'm sorry, Andrew. And I apologize to the rest of you as well. It's not my intention to be an asshole. I'm under a lot of stress, and I took it out on you. Please forgive me."

Everyone looked at Andrew, understanding it was his apology to accept or not. Even Nat, who knew him best, wasn't sure how her friend would respond. He was exhausted and probably in pain. To say he wasn't at his best would be the understatement of the year.

Andrew was silent a moment, but finally he smiled. "You're forgiven. This is hard enough without us at each other's throats. And you *are* a valuable member of the team, as long as you can stop being such an asshole."

Nat held her breath, but Steven came forward to shake Andrew's hand. "Done. I was genuinely worried for you, even though I'm sure it didn't come across that way. We're going to have to ensure you get the nutrients you need. Otherwise, with the frigid temperatures and the altitude, this will be extremely dangerous for you."

"That's okay. I'm not really a vegetarian. I just said that so you'd lay off Joe and Anubha."

"Wow, I really *have* been an asshole."

Igor clapped the mountaineer on the shoulder, and Nat noticed Steven didn't so much as shift his stance. It was probably a good thing the argument hadn't come down to a physical confrontation. She was no longer sure the Russian would have won. "Yah, you have been, but that is all over now. Now, we feast on plastic spaghetti, yes?"

The group laughed, and Nat watched the tension leave their gathering as if an actual cloud had disappeared. She resolved to sit beside Steven at lunch and get a handle on what was stressing him out.

As much as he gave her the creeps, it was her job to take care of these things.

However, Lana beat her to it. "What's bothering you, Steven? Anything we can do to help?"

He shook his head. "You'll laugh at me if I tell you."

"No, we won't." Lana's insistence was accompanied by assenting murmurs from the rest of the team. "What's going on?"

"How much do you all know about the Dyatlov group? I mean, *really* know about them?" Steven paced beside the fire, looking at each of them in turn.

Joe shrugged. "I know the basics. Nine Russian skiers went missing around here, and a search team found their bodies a week or two later. So far, no one knows for sure how they died, though some think it was an avalanche."

"The avalanche theory doesn't make any sense. It wasn't the right time of year or the right place. Plus, there were no signs of an avalanche, none of the damage you'd expect to see done to their tent or campsite," Lana said.

Steven nodded. "She's right. Anyone know some of the other theories?"

"Being Russian, this is a big deal to us. I think I have heard them all." Igor ticked them off on his fingers. "Weapons testing, government conspiracy, UFOs, animals, the wind going around the mountain made them crazy, the Mansi..." He tipped his head at Vasily, who was listening with no expression on his face. "Sorry."

"You did pretty well. But you're missing one. Do you remember what it is?"

"Wasn't it Bigfoot or something?" Anubha said, and Igor snickered.

"Oh yah, *Bigfeet*. I forgot about him."

"You're close. Not Bigfoot, but the yeti. Otherwise known as the abominable snowman." Out of everyone, Steven was the only one not smiling, but Nat had grown accustomed to that.

"So ridiculous." Anubha rolled her eyes. "Aliens? Bigfoot? I'm sorry, *yetis*. Who believes that stuff?"

"I do," Steven said. In the resulting silence, you could have heard a snowflake fall.

"You're joking, right?" Joe asked, but Nat could tell he wasn't. The mountaineer's face was so grave it could have been cast in stone.

"I told you you'd laugh."

"We're not laughing, Steven. It's a surprise, that's all. You seem so..." Lana trailed off.

"What, sane? Level-headed?"

"Serious, is what I was going to say."

"I am serious. My beliefs do not preclude that."

"So, what do you believe in? UFOs, yetis, or all of the above?" Andrew asked.

"I can't speak to UFOs, although I do think it's incredibly self-centered of us to think we're the only planet with intelligent life—using 'intelligent' very loosely in regard to our species. But that's par for the course, isn't it? Human beings are extremely self-centered. We have no concern for anything but ourselves."

Aaaand, just like that, Steven was back to being the happy soul they'd grown to know and love. "That's a cheery thought."

He pinned her to the spot with that alarmingly intense gaze of his. "No, Nat, it's downright depressing. But that doesn't make it any less true."

"So, it's yetis. That you believe in?" Igor said.

"Yes, but hear me out. I have my reasons. A few years ago, I was hiking in the Six Rivers National Forest, near the Oregon border. As usual, I was on my own, which didn't bother me. I actually prefer it that way."

It was difficult not to roll her eyes. Big surprise there.

"Anyway, it didn't take long for me to realize I *wasn't* alone. Something was tracking me. At first, I thought it was a wild animal, but it was too intelligent. Whatever was following me was capable of critical thinking. And it had opposable thumbs."

"Whaa?" Lana said. "How could you tell?"

"At night I kept my supplies up in the trees, in a net, and when I woke up, my pack had been rummaged through and every scrap of food that wasn't canned was gone. Here's the strange part—whatever went through my stuff had *untied* the net and unfastened my pack without damaging it or making enough noise to wake me up. What kind of wild animal is capable of that?"

"So it was a person," Andrew said, echoing Nat's own thoughts.

"That was my suspicion too, so the next night I set up a camera. And trust me, what I found on it the next morning was *not* human."

Nat shivered in spite of herself. Asshole or not, the man could tell a story.

"Are you saying you have the Bigfeet on video?" Igor asked, eyebrows disappearing under his fleece cap.

"Yes, I do. I suspected it was a hoax, some wiseass wearing a costume so he could steal from campers, so I brought it to these video production guys I know. Then I showed it to a few zoologists. They all confirmed it. This was no hoax."

"But if you have genuine footage of Bigfoot, it would be priceless," Nat said. "You'd be famous."

"That kind of fame I do not want."

"So what did you do with it?" Anubha asked. "Just put it in a drawer somewhere?"

"No, it's far too precious for that. Let's just say I've got it somewhere safe, somewhere no one will ever find it."

"But why? That kind of evidence, if it exists, could change everything." Andrew raised an eyebrow at her. Nat guessed his thoughts. If they could convince Steven to let them publicize it, what a podcast that would be. The resulting glory could lead to a lot more than a raise.

"Oh, it exists. But the way it would change things is exactly what I don't want."

"What do you mean?" Lana asked, but Nat was pretty sure she knew where the mountaineer was going with this. It was in his comments about the destructive nature of their species.

"Think about it. Once I released my evidence, people would descend on that forest, searching for him. In the process, they'd destroy one of the most beautiful wild spaces we have left. And if they found the creature? They'd destroy him too, all in the name of science."

"What kind of track did it leave?" Joe tipped his head at his wife, who handed him the bowls so he could fill them with steaming spaghetti. It looked and smelled every bit as good as what you'd order from an Italian restaurant. Nat's mouth watered.

"That's the thing. Aside from its immense stature, that's how I knew, without a doubt, that this wasn't some dumb animal. The creature wore a type of homemade shoe that looked like bits of plant and bark strapped to its feet. It made a kind of drag mark on the ground that could have been anything. It certainly wasn't as distinctive as a footprint."

The group fell silent, pondering the notion of a Sasquatch wearing shoes. It was an incredible story, but Nat didn't think the mountaineer was lying. Either he'd seen what he said, or he believed he'd seen it.

"Just because you saw this thing in the United States does not mean it's here, in Russia," Igor said.

"Are you aware of the note the searchers found in Dyatlov's tent?" Steven asked.

Nat was, and she felt chilled in a way that had nothing to do with the cold.

"It said, *From now on we know that snowmen exist.*"

~ CHAPTER FIVE ~

That evening, Nat found it impossible to sleep. It wasn't the cold. Andrew had done his research well, and even when the temperature plunged to -13°F, it was nice and cozy inside their two-person tent.

After Steven had told his story, a sense of dread had followed her around that couldn't be shaken by exhaustion, exercise, or the two hot meals expertly prepared by Joe and Anubha.

"Nat?" She wasn't surprised when Andrew whispered her name, but she still jumped.

"Yeah?"

"What did you think of that story?"

"I thought it was pretty fucking creepy. Especially that part about the shoes."

Andrew was silent for so long she thought he'd fallen asleep, but then he spoke. "Yeah. The shoes. You're thinking about Dyatlov, aren't you?"

Obviously she was thinking of Dyatlov. By tomorrow afternoon, they would reach the man's campsite. "One of the reasons no one believed the yeti theory—"

"In addition to the fact it's ridiculous."

"—is that there weren't any tracks. But maybe there *were* tracks. They just weren't recognizable."

"You realize how crazy this is."

But was it? They'd investigated far crazier. What about the bridge that drove animals to commit suicide? They'd never been able to find a rational explanation for that, either. Their entire podcast was based on the fact that sometimes there was no rational explanation.

"If there is something like that out here, it's not even supernatural. It's a creature that hasn't been discovered yet. Aren't scientists discovering new species every day?" Nat's heart picked up speed. What if they returned with proof—actual proof—that yetis existed? She wouldn't be as reticent as their mountaineering friend, that was for sure.

"Yeah, but that's like bugs and stuff, not carnivores. Trust me, if something like that existed, someone would have seen it by now."

"There have been lots of sightings."

"And not one of them verified."

"What about Steven's?" Nat asked.

"What *about* Steven's? We haven't seen it. We only have his word for it."

Her producer had a point. Still…

"I believe him."

"I kind of do as well. Which is why I can't sleep."

"Andy?"

"Mmm-hmm?"

"Do you think we're going to be okay? I mean, what happened to the Dyatlov group won't happen to us, will it?"

"Definitely not. That was sixty years ago. Even if there were creatures living up here back then, I'm sure they've moved on by now. And the Cold War is over." Andrew had always leaned toward the government-conspiracy side of things.

"That note has always freaked me out, though."

"Me too. I wonder why he didn't mention—"

"The photograph? Yeah, I wondered that as well. Maybe he doesn't know about it?" Though that was unlikely. Steven appeared to be an expert on the subject.

One of the skiers' cameras had been left behind in a tent. When the film was developed, a single photo of a large, humanoid figure, dark against the tree line, had been discovered.

It was enough to give one nightmares. Some believed it was one of the other skiers in a snowsuit—the figure was too shadowy to make out any details, even with enhancement—but there was something otherworldly, something not quite right about it.

"*I'm going to fucking kill you!*"

"What the hell—"

Getting out of her sleeping bag wasn't easy. It encased her like a cocoon, and she realized for the first time how vulnerable it made her. There would be no such thing as a fast escape.

The sound of zippers and nylon rustling filled the night. Apparently, everyone had the same idea.

"Andy, help."

Her producer took hold of her upper body around the shoulders and pulled until Nat could finally kick her legs free. Yanking on their boots, they burst outside in their thermals to find the rest of the group watching Joe. The formerly mild-mannered Canadian brandished a filleting knife with a wicked blade, his eyes black with hatred.

"What's going on?" Andrew asked, and Nat realized everyone except the Mansi was standing in the snow, in freezing temperatures, in their thermals.

That was how easy it was to get everyone to leave their tents in their underwear, even when it was fifteen degrees below zero. Someone needed to create a diversion, and that was all it took. She shuddered at the thought. At least they hadn't sliced open their tent, but that was a small comfort.

"I'm going to kill that fucker, that's what's going on," Joe yelled, lunging toward Igor, who raised his hands in surrender. Igor? What had Igor done?

But then Lana lifted her lantern and Nat saw who was behind Igor. Steven. It figured.

"No one's killing anyone. Let's try to calm down. Can somebody tell me what happened, please?" Andrew's voice was steady, which Nat found admirable, because Joe looked like he wasn't too choosy about how he used his knife at the moment.

"I don't know. We heard yelling and came outside to find Joe about to murder Steven." Lana's hand trembled, making the light dance. She was the only one wearing her coat.

"The fucker deserves it. No one messes with my wife."

Anubha appeared from the darkness to lay a hand on Joe's arm. "I'm sure it was a joke. It's not worth it, Joe. Let's go back to bed."

"No, I've had it. We've put up with enough abuse as it is, and I didn't sign up to be in this godforsaken place with a fucking psycho." He shook her off and took a menacing step toward Steven. Igor stood his ground, but it was obvious to Nat how quickly this could go wrong. Joe was lithe and agile. If he wanted to dart around the big Russian to get at Steven, he would. The mountaineer would be gutted before the rest of them registered what had happened.

"Someone please tell me what happened. I can't help if I don't know what's wrong. Igor?" Nat appealed to the Russian as Steven's tent mate, since Joe was clearly incapable of rational discussion.

Not taking his eyes from Joe, Igor shrugged. "I have no idea. One minute, we are sleeping; the next minute, Joe attacks our tent."

Joe's eyes narrowed. "That fucker wasn't sleeping."

For once, the mountaineer looked nervous, keeping the Russian between him and the Canadian. "I have no idea what he's talking about. I swear to God, Nat. I was sound asleep before he pulled me out here."

"Joe, please tell us what's wrong. Why are you so upset with Steven?" The Canadian was still breathing hard, plumes of smoke swathing his face in a silvery fog, but the arm that brandished the knife had lowered. Clinging to her belief that the trapper was a reasonable man, Nat focused her energy on him. "I promise you, if he upset you or Anubha, he'll be on the next plane home tomorrow. But I need you to tell me what happened."

The cold bit into her skin through the light silk of her thermals. Nat stomped her feet to keep the blood running. Soon she would have to go back to her tent, at least to get properly dressed.

Joe continued to glare in the mountaineer's direction, his body coiled to strike. Time was running out to save the man's life. There was only so long Igor could shield him.

"Joe, he isn't worth it. Do you really want to go to prison for the rest of your life over this? What about Anubha? What about your children? Do you want them to see you in jail? Let's talk about this."

Anubha tugged on her husband's arm again and Nat winced, fearing the man might lash out at her. He certainly looked furious enough. "Come on, Joe. Let's go back to bed. It was just a prank. Nat is right; he isn't worth it."

This time, the trapper lowered his arm all the way. He spat on the snow. "If you come after us again, I'll kill you, I swear to God. If it were just the two of us here tonight, you'd already be dead."

"I don't know what happened to upset you, but it couldn't have been anything I did. I was asleep. Igor can vouch for me." Now that the worst of the crisis had passed, Steven stepped around the big Russian. "I may be a prick, but I give you my word I'd never do anything to you or your wife."

Nat appealed to Anubha, who seemed a lot calmer than her husband. "What happened?"

The woman moved into the lantern light to lay a blanket around her husband's shoulders, and Nat noticed her eyes were glittering with tears.

"Something woke me up. This horrible, heavy breathing, something snuffling around my head. It sounded so close, like it was right on the other side of our tent, so I sat up, and that's when it growled." Her voice broke. "It scared me to death."

"Sounds like an animal," Andrew said.

"It was no fucking animal. When I turned on the lantern, I saw its silhouette. It stood tall like a man." Joe's hands clenched into fists, his blade catching the light and winking ominously. "And there's only one man here sick enough to play a joke like that."

"Joe, I can understand why you're upset. If someone frightened my partner like that, I'd be angry too. But Steven doesn't strike me as a prank-playing kind of guy," Andrew said.

"That's because I'm not. I've never played a prank in my life, especially something like that. It's so important we get our rest for the climb tomorrow. I would never mess with that." Steven wrapped his arms around his upper body and stamped his feet, and that's when Nat saw he wasn't even wearing his boots. He was in his wool socks. Since Joe had dragged him from his tent, she guessed that made sense. "If I've given you folks the impression I want to sabotage this expedition, I apologize. Because nothing could be further from the truth."

"You were the only one talking about fucking yetis. No one else believes in that shit." Joe spat on the snow again.

"That doesn't mean I'd pretend to be one. Jesus Christ. I'm not insane."

"Did you hear it growl, Joe?" Lana asked.

The trapper shook his head. "No, I slept through it. Anubha woke me up."

"I was scared to death. I've never heard anything like it in my life." The trapper sobbed, and Nat felt intensely sorry for her. Whether it had been a hoax or not, it would have been an awful way to wake up. She'd once gone on an African safari and heard a leopard growl outside her tent. While the creature had actually been some distance away, it had sounded close enough to touch. She'd never forget how terrifying that had been.

"Did anyone check for tracks?" she asked.

"Didn't even think of it," Joe said. "I knew who it was."

Steven opened his mouth, but Nat held up her hand to cut him off before the argument got heated again. "Let's say Steven's telling the truth. It's worth a look, isn't it?"

"I think we should all get some gear on first. Otherwise, we're going to freeze," the mountaineer said. "The last thing we want is for history to repeat itself."

Weak with relief, Nat headed to her tent as fast as her frozen feet could carry her. Andrew followed, and they knocked into each other in their rush to pull on snow pants, parkas, and caps.

"This is so bizarre," her producer muttered, keeping his voice low. "Not to get melodramatic, but this expedition seems fucking cursed."

"No more so than anything else involving people. People always complicate things."

"True, but Joe was ready to *murder* Steven. Like, seriously slit his throat. I really think that guy would be dead if Igor hadn't intervened."

"Something has to be done to release the tension in this group before it explodes. Whenever I think we're okay, something else happens to put us at each other's throats again. If this continues, I think we should call it a day."

"Are you serious?" Andrew raised an eyebrow. "But Nat, all that money. All that time. And the listeners…"

"I know. They won't be happy. But it is what it is. I'm not going to risk people's lives for a story."

"We better get back out there before they give up on us. We'll talk about this later."

The rest of their group was already clustered around the back of Joe and Anubha's tent. There was almost a reverential feel to the gathering; everyone circled around a single light with their heads lowered as if in prayer.

Nat gently pushed her way into the circle. "What is it? Did you find anything?"

"See for yourself," Steven said. Maybe it was a trick of the light, but the mountaineer's tan skin appeared ashen.

She studied the snow outside the tent. It was smooth and unblemished.

There wasn't a single track.

~ CHAPTER SIX ~

It was a somber group that set off for the Dyatlov Pass the next morning. Even Lana and Igor were silent, focused on the terrain ahead. When Nat suggested the Russian bring up the rear this time, the man had shrugged and fallen back without a word of complaint. She couldn't tell if he was bothered by it or not.

As though to match their mood, the temperature had fallen considerably. Soon the effort of negotiating the challenging climb in skis warmed her, but Nat worried about what would happen when they stopped and the sweat froze, chilling her further. At least her expensive gear wicked the moisture away from her skin, but the idea of being encased in several thin layers of ice didn't thrill her.

Only Vasily appeared to be unaffected by the events of the night before, but whether that was because he'd slept through it all or hadn't bothered to leave his tent, she wasn't sure. He had watched them as they silently ate their miserable breakfast, refusing their food to chew on some kind of dry, leathery meat, as always, and then had taken the head of the trail once he saw they were ready to go.

"My wife isn't crazy."

"Huh?" Nat had been so focused on the path that she hadn't noticed Joe had dropped back to speak to her.

"I said, my wife isn't crazy. If she says something was outside our tent last night, something was outside our tent."

"Joe, no one is doubting Anubha. I believe she heard something, and I believe you saw something. I just don't think it was Steven."

"Who else would it be?"

Nat was saddened to see the amiable hunter hadn't regained his equilibrium. He was still angry, still on the offensive. "I'm sorry I don't have an answer for you. But I don't believe it was anyone in the group. No one here would do something like that."

"There's no other explanation. Either you think Anubha is crazy, or someone was outside our tent last night."

"You said you saw its silhouette? That it stood tall, like a man?"

"Yeah."

"Maybe it was a bear. Vasily said there are bears around here."

"A bear that doesn't leave tracks? Besides, bears hibernate."

"Steven would have left tracks too," Nat said.

"Maybe not. Maybe the fucker got rid of them somehow. You heard his story about Bigfoot's shoes."

They lapsed into silence, the only sound the swish of Nat's skis, her labored breathing, and the crunch of Joe's walking stick breaking through the snow. It would have been tempting to write off Anubha's experience as a nightmare, but Joe *had* seen something outside their tent. Nat wished she had an explanation for him, but, failing that, she still couldn't believe it was Steven. Aside from the fact he'd been inside his tent when Joe attacked him, it wasn't in the man's nature to pull something like this.

"Maybe someone else did it as a joke, like Anubha said, and now they're too scared to admit it."

"Who, Lana? Vasily? Igor was fast asleep until I went for that creep."

"But Steven was as well, wasn't he?"

Joe sneered. "He was faking it."

"How would he have gotten back into his tent, never mind into his sleeping bag, before you came out and got him?"

"I had to find my knife. It gave him a head start."

"Yeah, about that. I understand you were upset, but we can't go around threatening each other with knives. If you have a problem with someone, please talk to Andrew or me about it, and we'll resolve it. We can't have anyone murdered on our watch."

"I'm sorry; I lost my temper. That guy gets under my skin."

"I know; he gets under mine as well. But I really don't think he's to blame this time."

"Don't tell me you believe in yetis too."

From now on we know that snowmen exist.

"It has to be someone from our group playing a prank. I don't know who, and I doubt we'll ever find out. Who would admit it now?"

"Anubha said it didn't sound human."

Dread ran icy fingers along Nat's spine, but she shook them off, doing her best to keep her imagination from running away with her. "Maybe it was an animal, an animal too light to leave tracks." She gestured at Joe's feet. The snow was packed firmly enough that his snowshoes rarely broke the surface. "Is it possible the shadow you saw was a trick of the light?"

"It was a man. No way it was an animal."

She wished it *had* been Steven. That at least was a benign explanation. "Vasily was the only one who didn't come out of his tent last night."

"Vasily? What reason would he have for doing something like this?"

"I don't know. I get the feeling he doesn't think we should be here. Maybe he's trying to scare us."

"But if the expedition ends early, his pay would be cut short too, won't it? He wouldn't sacrifice that. Now that he's here, I think he's resigned to see it through."

Was he? Nat wasn't so sure. She didn't like the way the Mansi had been conveniently absent whenever shit was going down. Perhaps he was trying to stay out of it, but his obvious disapproval grated on her. She wouldn't have put it past him to sabotage the expedition.

What a mess. Who was she supposed to trust? At least she had Andrew.

At that moment, Igor yelled from behind them, startling her so much she nearly lost her balance. "Help! Help, I need help."

Nat turned to see her dearest friend lying facedown in the snow.

* * *

The Mansi frowned. "This no good. I must go back, get help."

Even though she didn't trust him, the idea of Vasily leaving them alone on the pass terrified her. "No, if you leave, we all do. We can't stay here without you. It's not safe."

"I'm okay. I'll be fine. It was just low blood sugar." Andrew's head was propped on Lana's lap, in front of an impromptu campfire Igor and Steven had started. Since he'd regained consciousness, he'd been sucking back electrolyte packets like nobody's business, and Nat had to admit he did look a lot better.

"You don't know that, Andrew. You could have had a heart attack," Lana said. "You need to see a doctor. This is too dangerous."

"If it were a heart attack, he wouldn't have recovered so quickly." Steven took off his glove to lay his hand on Andrew's chest. After a moment, he shook his head. "It feels normal. Slow, steady. It wasn't a heart attack. Probably a combination of low blood sugar, stress, and exhaustion."

"Are you willing to stake his life on that? Because I'm not." Lana held her hand to Andrew's forehead, narrowing her eyes, as if daring Steven to take him away from her. "Doesn't anyone have any medical training?"

"Only what I've learned in the bush, but I agree with Steven, for what it's worth. I don't think it was a heart attack," Anubha said.

Nat watched them debate the health of her friend, unable to speak, though inside she was screaming. If something happened to him, if he died because of her, because of this stupid expedition, she'd never forgive herself.

"I don't think we should take the chance. Lana's right; it's too risky." Joe put his arm around his wife, looking down at Andrew. It drove Nat crazy to see how people were staring at him, as though he were some strange species of bug under a microscope.

"I'm fine, honest. I think I needed rest, is all. How much farther is it to the site?" Andrew asked.

Steven reached for his GPS, but the Mansi beat him to it. "About an hour, maybe two. But it's all uphill."

"Maybe we could make some kind of litter and carry him." Steven looked at the other men for affirmation. "He doesn't seem that heavy."

"You don't have to *carry* me. This is silly. I got dizzy and passed out. That's it. It's not like my leg is broken or anything. I need to take it a little easier, is all." Andrew finished another electrolyte packet, handing the empty container to Lana. "Christ, this is embarrassing."

"Nat, this is really your call. What do you want to do?"

Steven's question startled her from her inertia. "I think we should turn back."

"No, Nat. We can't. Please don't call it quits because of me. Please." Andrew's eyes pleaded with her, but she refused to let him sway her. "You haven't even interviewed anyone yet."

"I'm sorry, Andy, but I'm not going to risk your life for some stupid podcast. It's not worth it."

"Going down the pass could be more dangerous, though. Vasily's right—it's probably best if he goes for help while the rest of us stay put. If there is something wrong with Andrew's heart and he collapses out here…" Steven didn't finish his thought, but he didn't need to. The idea of it was enough to make Nat feel like screaming again.

"Jesus Christ, there's nothing wrong with my heart. I got a physical before we left. Clean bill of health. I just overdid it today."

"What did you feel like before you passed out?" Anubha asked.

"Dizzy. I couldn't catch my breath, and I couldn't focus. My vision went black, and there were little dots in front of my eyes."

"Any chest pain, or pain through the arms? Any pressure right here?" She tapped her fingers against her breastbone.

"None. I felt dizzy for a moment, and then boom! I was out."

"It doesn't sound like a heart attack. Sometimes the altitude can get a bit much for people, because the air is thinner. But you're from California, not the Plains. It should be easier for you."

"Maybe I wouldn't have made it *this* far if I were from the Plains. My usual exercise is running my mouth. Tell them, Nat."

If Andrew was back to cracking jokes, he probably wasn't on death's door. Nat forced a smile, but it felt weak. Her own heart rate hadn't returned to normal yet. "He does go to the gym, but mostly for window shopping."

Lana laughed, but Steven had a blank expression that indicated her wit had gone over his head. No surprise there. "Even if we decide to send Vasily back to the village, it's getting too late. I suggest a few of us go on ahead and set up camp at the site. Once everything's in place, I'll return to help with Andrew," he said.

"I feel a million times better. I think I'll be fine getting to the site under my own power." To prove it, Andrew sat up, but Nat didn't miss the wince he tried to hide. Shit. She'd prepared for nicks, cuts, and bruises, but hadn't anticipated a life-threatening illness. The dread she'd felt since arriving in Russia pressed heavier on her shoulders.

"That is too much work, Steven. Me and the others can handle Andrew," Igor said, and unless she was mistaken, he sounded offended. No wonder—Andy wasn't a large man. The Russian could probably carry him up the mountain by himself if he had to.

Steven shrugged. "Suit yourself, but whoever's going to set up camp needs to get going. It'll be dark before we know it."

"I'll go with you," Anubha said. "It would be good to get some traps in place before nightfall."

As the three prepared to leave, Nat was overwhelmed with melancholy, as if she'd never see them again. Steven and Vasily were necessary evils, but she actually liked the Inuit tracker. She hugged Anubha tightly, her mind straying to the Dyatlov group, and how they'd met their doom separately. Had splitting up caused their demise? If they'd stayed together, would they have survived? It was impossible to say.

"Be careful," she said.

"Always. Don't worry. I'll see you in a couple of hours." Anubha patted her on the back, kissed her husband goodbye, and strapped on her snowshoes. Nat watched the trio ascend until they vanished from view, praying her misgivings were the product of an overactive imagination, nothing more.

"We should start soon. We do not want to fall too far behind the others." Igor knelt next to Andrew. "Do you feel well enough to ski? If not, I can carry you."

Nat hoped her producer would be honest. Now was not the time for false bravado.

"I'm still a little weak, but I'd like to try. I am feeling a lot better than I was earlier."

Reaching out to the Russian, Andrew allowed Igor to lift him into a standing position. Nat held her breath while she waited to see if her friend would regain his equilibrium or collapse. After a moment, he grinned, though his voice was shaky.

"All right. Let's blow this popsicle stand."

Lana tugged on Nat's sleeve. "Can I speak with you privately for a moment?"

Nat nodded. "We'll be right there," she told the others before allowing the Olympian to lead her away from the fire. The harsh reality of the dropping temperature hit her as soon as she left the warmth of the flames. Getting to camp would soon be a matter of life and death, not only for Andrew, but for all of them. "What is it?"

"I'm worried about your friend. I don't mean to scare you, but I don't think this is a matter of him being tired or out of shape. I'm afraid he might have altitude sickness."

"What? But Kholat Syakhl's peak isn't eight thousand feet. It's too low."

"This isn't only about the altitude. It's how fast we've been traveling and the fact he's out of condition. Out of condition for this kind of climbing, I mean. He's still out of breath while he's resting, and that's not normal, even on Everest. If he pushes himself to keep ascending now, it might kill him."

Looking closely at her friend, Nat could see how he gasped for air, though he tried hard to hide it. The idiot was going to get himself killed. "What do we do?"

"I'm assuming there is no canned oxygen available?"

Nat, while never the most organized person at the best of times—she often teased Andrew about being the "brains of the operation"—wanted to shrink into her parka in shame. Her cheeks burned. "It never occurred to me we'd need it for this little of an incline. I feel so stupid."

Lana patted her arm. "Don't. It's not your fault. No one could have seen this coming. Without oxygen, the best thing to do would be to rest here for a couple of days, long enough to let his body adjust to the altitude. You might be able to get away with one, but I wouldn't push it. Altitude sickness can be fatal."

As the reality of what Lana said sunk in, Nat felt a chill that had nothing to do with the arctic air. "We can't stay here by ourselves. What if his condition gets worse? It would be suicide."

"I agree. I'm glad you're taking this seriously. I'd hate to see something happen to Andrew. He's a great guy."

Nat shoved aside the idea of anything happening to her friend, unable to contemplate the possibility without completely losing it. "Yes, he is. So, will you stay with us?"

"I would in a heartbeat, but I think it would be better if you had some muscle here, just in case, and there's no way Joe will agree to be separated from his wife, especially after what happened last night. So that leaves Igor."

But would the Russian go for it? That was the question. While he wasn't as competitive as Steven, Nat couldn't see him thrilled at the prospect of being stuck here with the two lame ducks.

"I'm fine with that, if he's willing."

Lana smiled. "I'm sure he will be. Let's go ask him."

As Nat suspected, Igor was not an enthusiastic volunteer. He didn't say much, but he didn't have to. His reluctance was written all over his face. Andrew put up a brief protest until he realized there was no way he could convince them he was fine to continue the ascent. With a sigh, he lowered himself to the ground in front of the fire. Nat could have sworn he looked relieved.

"Since you're staying here, you get your pick of the meals," Joe said, holding out the foil packages like an oversized deck of cards. "Take a few, in case you have to stay for a couple of days. I have an extra folding pot, so I'll leave that with you as well."

"Thanks, Joe." She left Igor in charge of the menu selection, and the Russian's discriminating tastes resulted in pad Thai, beef stroganoff, and some weird breakfast wrap thing.

"Are you sure you're going to be all right? I don't feel good about leaving you here." Nat was touched by Joe's concern, though she also knew he would never abandon his wife.

"We'll be fine. We have Igor. We'll set up camp, make some dinner, and turn in early. I'm sure Andy will feel better tomorrow."

"Well, let me help you with the tents. It's the least I can do."

"You'd better get moving. It's sunny now, but the afternoon will go by quickly," Igor said.

"I insist. Come on, Lana, give us a hand."

Though she felt guilty, Nat was relieved when the tents were set up and their emergency pit stop resembled an official camp. It made her feel safer, and with her lack of experience, she hadn't relished stumbling around in the dark on her own.

"Take care of yourself, guys." Joe shook Igor and Andrew's hands and gave her a quick hug. "We'll probably see you tomorrow."

"See you tomorrow," Nat said.

She wished it didn't sound so ominous.

~ CHAPTER SEVEN ~

The wind picked up as the sun went down, howling through the peaks. It sounded like a wild animal, reminding Nat of the photo that had been discovered in Dyatlov's camera.

She drew closer to the fire, shivering. Now that Igor was resigned to staying behind, he had returned to his cheerful self, entertaining them both with bawdy stories. While Andrew was quieter than normal, his breathing was less pronounced, to the point she couldn't hear it anymore. She took that to be a positive sign.

Hard to believe that five hours away from them, the rest of their group was already recreating the movements of Igor Dyatlov and his companions. Nat wondered if any sign of the decades-old tragedy remained. Was the campsite disturbing, or peaceful? Had Steven pitched his tent in the same location as Dyatlov's? Were the treetops still burned? It was difficult to be so close, and yet so far, from the action.

Her wistfulness drove her to talk about it. Pulling out her gear, she initiated her first interview for the podcast. "What do you think happened, Igor?"

She didn't have to elaborate. The Russian answered so quickly it was as though he'd been waiting to be asked. "I think it was the government. Yah, the radiation, the strange injuries, it makes sense. I think they stumbled onto a secret weapons-testing site and saw something they weren't supposed to see."

"I used to believe the same thing. But now that I'm out here, I don't know. Those theories about the infrasound caused by the wind or avalanche paranoia making them crazy—I could see it," Andrew said.

Igor laughed, though Nat could tell Andy wasn't joking. "Are you going a little insane, my friend?"

"Not yet. At least, I don't think so, but if I were, I'd probably be the last to know. Look at our group, for example."

Nat had a feeling she knew where this was going, but had to ask anyway. She stopped recording. "What do you mean?"

"Last night, Anubha heard something outside her tent, and based on nothing but a hunch, Joe was willing to kill Steven over it. I don't know about you guys, but he strikes me as a fairly levelheaded dude. People are already going crazy, and we aren't even at the Dyatlov site yet."

"That's far from the same thing. Steven has been getting on everyone's nerves from the beginning," she said.

"Enough to *kill* him over? Doesn't that seem a bit extreme?"

"It's extreme, yah, but you don't mess with a man's wife." Igor added more branches to the campfire, releasing a flurry of sparks.

"But that's what I'm saying. Steven didn't mess with Anubha. He was asleep in his tent, with you. You would have heard him if he'd left and come back in a hurry, right?"

Igor thought for a moment, using a long stick to stir the ashes amid the coals. "Yah, I think so."

"I watched him carefully during that entire exchange, and unless he's an Academy Award–winning actor in addition to being a highly skilled mountaineer, Joe blindsided him. Steven looked like someone who'd been startled out of a deep sleep by some bizarre crisis he didn't understand."

"What's your point, Andrew?" Nat asked, though she wasn't sure she wanted to know.

"My point is, Anubha heard something that sounded like a wild animal outside their tent last night. Joe, with no rhyme or reason, no method to his madness, decided that what she heard must have been Steven playing a prank. This apparently filled him with murderous rage, and even when he found Steven fast asleep in his tent, he refused to relinquish his delusion."

Igor's brow furrowed. "When you put it that way, it does sound weird."

"It's beyond weird. It makes absolutely no sense. Your wife hears a wild animal, and your first thought is that it must be this guy from California who you don't even know?"

"Joe saw a man's silhouette, remember? That's what told him it was someone from our group." Nat had hoped to never go over this again, at least not while they were still on the mountain. Because there wasn't a rational explanation. No one in their group had had the time to sneak behind Joe and Anubha's tent, scare her, erase their tracks, and then get back into their own tent and sleeping bag before they were confronted.

But if it hadn't been someone in their group, who was it?

"Maybe Joe saw a shadow, and maybe he didn't. It really doesn't matter," Andrew said. "Regardless of what he saw, his reaction was completely irrational."

"So what are you saying? That Joe is a loose cannon?" Nat shifted her weight on the log, growing uncomfortable with the direction the conversation was taking. The last thing she wanted was to talk about the other members of the group behind their backs, especially a guy she liked as much as Joe. It was one thing when it was only she and Andrew. Then it could be forgiven as shoptalk. But now Igor was privy to it too.

Then she had a horrible thought. What if the rest of the group were talking about *them*? The two weak links and their Russian babysitter.

She could only imagine what they'd say. Her cheeks grew hot at the thought of it.

"No, that's not what I'm saying at all. Joe strikes me as a thoughtful, methodical guy, not someone to fly off the handle. But he *did* fly off the handle."

"And so?" She really wished he'd get to the point. He certainly had recovered his wind.

"And so, if on the very first night on this mountain, the most rational member of our group snapped and almost murdered another man for doing something he obviously didn't do, what's going to happen to us the longer we stay here? What's happening to them now, with all those bad vibes surrounding them? If Steven were smart, he'd have stayed down here with us. You're not there to protect him now, Igor. What if Joe goes crazy again? Who's going to stop him?"

"Bad *vibes?*" Nat had never heard the like come out of her producer's mouth before. He was supposed to be the skeptical half of their equation.

Andrew brushed her off with a wave of his hand. "Bad vibes, bad karma, negative energy, whatever you want to call it. I could feel it as soon as we set foot on this mountain. But up there—up there, they must be swimming in it."

"That's ridiculous. It's your imagination, nothing more. It's because you know what happened up here. That would make anyone jump at shadows."

"It wasn't my imagination when Joe went crazy last night. Did you see Anubha's face? I'm willing to bet that was completely out of character for him. And what happened to the Dyatlov group wasn't my imagination, either. Something drove them out of their tent and something tore them apart."

"Let's talk about something else. You two are starting to freak me out," Igor said.

"Yeah, we shouldn't talk about Joe when he's not here to defend himself. Imagine if they're doing the same to us." Nat hoped they weren't, but then again, would it be so bad if it gave the team an opportunity to vent a little? She was sure sticking to such a slow pace had been frustrating for them, some more than others.

"Fine. Whatever. You asked for my theory, and I gave it to you." Andrew leaned back, propping his feet in front of the flames.

"That was your theory?" Nat couldn't resist poking at him a little. "What, that Joe went mad and murdered everyone?"

"Laugh at me if you want, but some places are just plain bad. You know it as well as I do. Remember Poveglia?" Andrew asked, eferencing the most haunted island in the world. Poveglia had been the subject of their most popular cast to date. Nothing supernatural had happened during their visit, but there was an oppressive sense of dread about the place that infected you until you felt you'd go out of your mind. "I knew it was evil, the same way I know this place is evil. I'm willing to bet the reason it's called Dead Mountain has nothing to do with the lack of game. People die here."

"Now you're scaring *me*." Nat rubbed her arms in a vain attempt to get rid of the goosebumps.

"I think we should be scared. Like Steven said, this isn't a celebration. We shouldn't be acting like it is."

"You two can talk about evil all night if you want. Me, I'm going to have a drink." Igor stood, stretching his hands so his knuckles popped. "Anyone want to join me?"

"Whatcha got?" Andrew asked.

"Andrew, are you sure that's the smartest idea? What if Lana's right, and you do have altitude sickness? I'm sure alcohol won't help."

"Alcohol never hurts," Igor said, the flickering firelight turning his grin sinister. Great, now she was the one imagining things. Fucking Andrew. She would probably have nightmares, and it would be his fault.

"If I'm going to die on this godforsaken mountain, I might as well enjoy whatever time I have left. Make it a double, Igor."

"Are you crazy? We drink from the bottle. Every man for himself. And maybe, every woman?"

"No thanks. One of us should retain control of her faculties." Nat glared at Andrew, but if he noticed, it didn't faze him. "I am *not* carrying either of you tomorrow, so keep that in mind."

"Jesus, Nat. It's one drink. When did you turn into such a pill? Don't know if you got the memo, but prohibition is over."

"Prohibition never started here," Igor said, to which both men guffawed like it was the funniest thing they'd ever heard. Perhaps the altitude was getting to them both.

When the Russian returned with his bottle of hooch, hoisting it in triumph, an unearthly howl split the night. It made the hairs on the back of Nat's neck rise, and she grabbed Andrew's leg and squeezed it without thinking.

"Hey!" he yelped, squirming to get away from her.

"What the fuck was that?"

Only Igor took it in stride. "Wolves."

"That was no fucking wolf. I know what a wolf sounds like," Andrew said.

"Russian wolves, they are different." Igor raised his hands to the sky. "My children of the night, what beautiful music they make."

"Beautiful music my ass."

Nat had to agree with Andrew. There had been nothing beautiful about that howl. It was entirely too close for comfort. "Do you think the rest of the group is all right?"

"Sure, they are all right. They have three powerful hunters. We have just each other. And this." Igor took a long drink from his bottle before handing it to Andrew.

"I'm really sorry for fucking everything up, Nat."

She patted Andrew's foot, the only thing that was within reach since he'd moved away from her. "You didn't fuck up anything."

"I did, though. It's my fault that we're here while the rest of the group is having a roaring good time." Turning the bottle over in his hands, he studied the clear liquid as if wanting to commit it to memory.

Nat pictured the dour Vasily, Steven the pessimist, and the tension that no doubt emanated from Joe. Though the separation increased her anxiety, in a way she was glad to get a break from them. So much drama. That was what always resulted when other people got involved with her projects. "I seriously doubt that. Have you met the rest of our group?"

Andrew laughed. "True. They're not exactly party-hearty types."

"We have the party right here. I brought it with me." Igor gestured to his bottle, which Andrew was still regarding like a museum specimen. "Drink up, my friends."

When Andrew passed the bottle to her, she took a long drink, the moonshine tracing a trail of fire down her throat to her belly.

Misery loved company, after all. And she was no party pooper.

~ CHAPTER EIGHT ~

Something was shaking her. Nat pried open her eyes and cried out when she saw the face looming over hers.

"Christ, you reek. Have you been *drinking*?"

Indignant, she propped herself up on her arms, glaring at the intruder. "Maybe. What are you doing here?"

"While you guys have been having yourselves a party, we've been going through hell. You have to get up there, Nat." Steven's face was unusually pale, his lips set in a thin, white line. He looked like he'd seen his own ghost.

"It's not that easy. What about Andrew? If he hasn't recovered from his altitude sickness, we can't move him."

"Then leave him here." Steven's tone left no doubt as to what he thought of her closest friend. If her feet hadn't been trapped in nylon, she would have kicked him. "But you've got to get up there right away. And bring Igor too. We could use him."

"I'm not abandoning Andrew. What's going on? What time is it, anyway?" It was gloomy inside the tent, with only enough light to cast half the mountaineer's face in shadow.

"Not sure. I left as soon as there was enough light to ski by. Five, six? Possibly later. The sun seems to rise later here."

Nat felt like she'd been run over by a horse-drawn cart and dragged for a couple of miles. Her mouth tasted of paste and bile. Lovely. She didn't doubt she reeked. The reality that Steven had taken the risk of skiing alone to their camp slowly sank in. "What happened? Is anyone hurt?"

His presence in her tent meant that Joe hadn't killed him, which she supposed was a relief. But had the trapper attacked someone else? "For God's sake, Steven, this is no time to keep me in suspense. Tell me what happened."

"We don't know if anyone is hurt or not. But Joe and Anubha are missing."

* * *

Her ragtag little group was decidedly more ragtag this morning than they'd been the day before. Nat didn't think any of them had drank much, certainly not enough to have had a hangover, but Igor's Russian hooch was strong. It wasn't doing them any favors.

She looked at Andrew one last time, paying careful attention to his breathing. He no longer sounded breathless, and his eyes had some of their old spark back, but she didn't want to take any chances. Lana would have insisted on giving him more recovery time, but desperation tended to blow caution out of the water. There was no way she would consider leaving him here by himself.

"Are you sure you're okay?"

"I'm fine, Nat. I promise. Don't worry about me. We have bigger problems right now."

She'd still worry about him, though. Of course she would.

The extra weight of her pack dug into her shoulders, making it more challenging to push off. She'd divided her producer's things between her, Steven, and Igor, hoping to ease Andrew's burden as much as possible. Her legs, which were already screaming at her, caught fire. She moaned under her breath.

Steven turned. "You doing all right?"

"I'm fine. Just sore." She wasn't going to complain about tired muscles, not when her dearest friend might be dying from altitude sickness or worse. *Please God, don't let him die. I'll even believe in you if you don't let him die.* "Can you tell me what happened?"

Steven shrugged. "Not much else to tell. The Canadians got into it a bit with Vasily yesterday, and sometime after that, about when everyone was getting ready to call it a night, we noticed they were missing."

"But—" Nat took a deep breath, forcing herself to speak slowly. Her lungs ached, and gulping the frozen air wasn't helping. "But what do you mean, they 'got into it a bit'? About what?"

She couldn't imagine anyone getting angry enough at Vasily to argue with him. For one, the man hardly spoke.

"He wouldn't let them set their traps. They didn't take too kindly to that. I wasn't real happy about it, either, to be honest. I could do with some fresh meat. This astronaut food is getting old."

"What do you mean, he wouldn't let them?" Nat tried to reconcile the image of the reticent man physically restraining either of the trappers and failed. "Did he sabotage their traps?"

"Oh no, nothing like that. If he had, it would have been him that went missing, I'm sure. But he went ballistic when he saw the traps, started screaming a bunch of stuff we didn't understand. And unfortunately, we didn't have Igor to translate."

Sound carried well in the mountains. "Wouldn't have mattered anyway," Igor yelled up at them. "He doesn't speak much Russian. The Mansi have their own dialect."

Nat took another breath of ice, her mind racing. "But Vasily speaks English. That's one of the reasons I hired him. Didn't he say *anything* you could understand?"

"Not much. He was too upset. Something about it being someone else's territory and they had no right. That's the most I got."

"Maybe they went to set their traps once Vasily wasn't looking. Or went hunting. Isn't that possible?" From what she'd seen of Anubha, the Canadian was a strong-willed woman. A woman who'd been hired for her hunting ability and survival skills. It was likely she hadn't let the Mansi tell her what to do.

"Sure, it's possible, but you'd think they would have been back by morning, or at least left word with one of us. I had Lana check on them at dawn—didn't want Joe to get the wrong idea after the other night—and it didn't look like anyone had slept in their tent. Their sleeping bags were untouched."

In spite of the admittedly grim scenario, Nat felt better. Anubha and Joe were more than capable of spending a few nights in the bush. That was why she'd hired them. They were independent, and as far as she'd seen, they'd formed no close ties with Lana. Certainly not with Steven or Vasily. Maybe if she'd been there, they would have felt an obligation to let her know where they were going and when they'd return. But she could see them not giving a rat's ass about alerting Steven.

It was inconsiderate, at the very least. But not an emergency. Yet.

"Why didn't anyone call me?" she asked. It would have been a hell of a lot easier than Steven coming back for their group.

"Everyone's been having trouble with their phones. Either we can't get a signal, or our batteries can't hold a charge. I'm hoping you brought a power pack that'll help."

"Yes, we've got four of them." They'd brought them for the podcast, but there was no reason why she couldn't use them to charge everyone's phones.

As the terrain grew increasingly difficult, even the mountaineer couldn't spare the wind to speak any longer. Nat was grateful. She felt light-headed and had to concentrate on placing one ski after the other on the treacherous slope. There was no brainpower to spare to worry about Anubha and Joe. *Trod, trod. Trod, trod.* The incline was wicked enough that there were few opportunities to glide. She and Andrew had practiced the wrong things. Their training was all but useless.

She could hear his breath becoming harsher behind her. Nightmare visions of his collapsing on the snow and not getting up this time made her entire body tremble. She struggled to find her footing. Finally, she had to stop.

"How is he?"

Igor had an arm around Andrew, and was half carrying her friend up the slope. Nat marveled at the Russian's strength, as he was also burdened with most of their supplies. "We will need to rest soon. His lungs, they are not so good."

"We're almost there," Steven said, his exhalations drawing pictures in the frosty air. "Only about a half mile left."

Nat groaned. Perhaps a half mile was nothing to the mountaineer, but for novice skiers who were ready to collapse, it might as well have been Nepal.

"You can do this." Once again, his eyes seemed to look right through her. "Come up here next to me. We'll do it together."

Once stopped, it took a Herculean effort to get going again, but somehow she found the strength to join Steven. He grasped her shoulder. "You all right?"

"Yeah. Just tired. I had no idea it was going to be so difficult."

"We'll be there before you know it. Focus on the landscape and how beautiful it is. It will take your mind off the pain."

Other than a blindingly blue sky, Nat didn't see what was so beautiful about it. Kholat Syakhl was stark and forbidding, an endless expanse of white snow and black rock beneath the peaks. Its coldness came from more than the temperature.

It truly was No Man's Land.

Steven managed a steady stream of chatter, which distracted her somewhat, but also increased her resentment. How was this so easy for him? Didn't it pose the slightest challenge? At least he didn't ask any questions. She might have mustered up the energy to drive her ski pole through his chest if he had.

The mountaineer was in the middle of a rant about how the 1996 Everest disaster had been preventable when something made him stop midsentence. "What the—"

At the sound of a woman's voice crying, "Thank God; thank God," Nat lifted her head. It was Lana, hurrying toward them from the opposite direction. Bizarrely, she wasn't wearing her skis. She ran over the trail in her boots, staggering and nearly falling with every step.

Though Nat hated to even think the word in reference to another woman, the Olympian appeared to be hysterical. Lana's hair was stringy and uncombed, her face red and streaked with tears.

"What are you doing? I told you we'd come straight back." Steven grasped her by the arms to keep her from falling. Clearly too upset to speak, she held him close and sobbed, her shoulders heaving.

Igor pushed past Nat, who turned just in time to support Andrew before he fell.

"Lana, what is wrong? What happened? Are you hurt?"

The Russian was no more successful in getting answers, and Nat struggled under Andrew's weight. "Steven, how much farther? I can't hold him much longer."

"Not far at all." Steven nudged the weeping woman toward Igor and rushed to help, earning serious brownie points as he lifted Andrew's weight from Nat's shoulders. For his part, Andrew was as malleable as a rag doll, not reacting as he was passed from one team member to another. "Igor, can you and Lana lead the way? We have to reach camp. Andrew needs to rest."

The Russian nodded, urging Lana forward, but she pushed away from him, stumbling off the trail and into deeper snow.

"No. No, I'm not going back there."

"What are you doing?" Nat could hear the frustration in Steven's voice, but it was obvious to her that Lana was in some kind of shock. She wasn't thinking clearly if she thought going off trail would prove to be any kind of salvation. "Lana, we have to get back."

The woman stopped thrashing through the snow long enough to meet their eyes. "I can't. There's too much blood. So much blood."

~ CHAPTER NINE ~

Trepidation overwhelmed her as she reached camp, almost expecting to see everything in black and white like the famous Dyatlov photos—the tent with its torn side, half-collapsed beneath a mound of snow. Instead, the vivid nylon of Steven and Joe's tents stood as a beacon against the whiteness, providing some welcome color. Nat was relieved to find they'd avoided the Dyatlov site entirely, pitching their tents on the other side.

The men had managed to convince Lana to accompany them, but the woman shook so severely Nat expected her to stop at any moment and refuse to go farther.

The camp was eerily quiet. She turned to Lana. "Where's Vasily? Did he leave too?" If he had, she would sue his ass off. He'd been hired to help them through this, goddammit, not take off at the first sign of trouble.

Lana gestured to the one tent made from natural materials. Heart pounding in her throat, Nat skied toward it. She didn't see any of the blood Lana had mentioned, but what if something had happened to the Mansi? What if the man's tent were a tomb?

"Vasily? Vasily, are you in there?"

She could have cried with relief when she immediately heard a shuffling within. Before long, a familiar weathered face emerged from the animal hides.

"We need to go, Miss. We have angered them."

"Angered who?" For the first time, Nat noticed how frightened the man was. He shrank back inside his shelter, obviously reluctant to leave it, and was even more gaunt than she'd remembered. She wasn't sure how it was possible for Vasily to have lost weight, but apparently he had. The man was a living shadow.

"The ones who rule this mountain. We must leave."

Nat looked to where Igor and Steven were attending to Andrew and Lana, helping them to sit around the dying fire. The pile of collected branches would be enough to get the blaze going again, but more would need to be gathered before nightfall if they were to stay warm. A lot more. It would take a collective effort to keep the fire going.

"We can't leave. Andrew is ill, possibly with altitude sickness. He needs to rest for at least a few days. Lana is in shock. And Anubha and Joe are missing."

The man peered at her from the darkness of his tent, the naked terror in his eyes unnerving. "Not missing. Dead. It is my fault."

Nat thought of Steven's account of a heated argument between Vasily and the trappers. Had it gotten even more heated after the mountaineer had left? "Did you hurt them, Vasily?"

"No, not me. Not me. But they didn't listen to my warning. They didn't believe. I should have tried harder."

"What warning?"

"No one can hunt on this land. It is their territory. We have no rights here."

She resisted the urge to seize him by the shoulders and shake him, but just barely. "*Whose* territory?"

The Mansi said a word she didn't understand, his eyes rolling around like those of a spooked horse.

"I'm sorry; I don't understand."

"The snowmen. This land belongs to the snowmen."

Nat shivered. *From now on we know that snowmen exist.* Could it be? After six decades? Clearly the Mansi wasn't joking, but there was no way he could be referring to the same creature referenced in the Dyatlov note. She touched the man's arm. "We can't leave, Vasily. At least not tonight. And we need your help. Please help us get the fire going again."

For a moment, she thought he would refuse, but after disappearing into his shelter, Vasily returned in his heavy, fur-lined jacket, emerging to stand beside her. "If we don't leave, they will kill us. The trappers disrespected them."

Vasily's fear was contagious, his terror getting to her like a damp cold sinks into one's bones. "There's a chance Andrew will be well enough to leave in the morning. Do you think we'll be okay for the night?"

The man shrugged. "It is impossible to say. Perhaps if we leave them a peace offering, it will give us more time."

"Then we'll do that. In the meantime, please help us with the fire."

Nat followed her guide to the others, mind racing. Already the fire had been replenished enough to revive her, thawing her cheeks with its warmth. She was filled with gratitude as she removed her skis, laying the poles beside them. If she never skied again in her lifetime, that would be fine with her.

Lowering herself to the makeshift log bench where Andrew and Lana huddled together, she took her friend's hand and squeezed it. "How are you feeling?"

"Exhausted, but Lana doesn't want me to sleep yet. Just in case."

Nat studied him with what she hoped was a critical eye, wishing she'd found the time to take more than a basic first aid class. His color was good, his breathing steady, but his eyelids were at half-mast. He clearly needed to rest.

"Are you nauseous?" She ran over the symptoms of altitude sickness in her mind. "Do you feel disoriented in any way?"

"No, only tired. Really, really tired."

"Lana, is it okay if Andrew lies down for a bit? He needs to rest."

The Olympian's eyes were glazed and dull. "Not yet. Someone needs to monitor his breathing."

Feeling helpless, Nat rubbed her friend's hands to get the blood flowing. What a mess. What a colossal mess. Andrew was ill, Lana was in questionable shape, and the guide Nat had hired to protect them was ranting about snowmen. The trappers were missing, presumably along with most of the group's food supplies. The situation couldn't possibly be any worse.

"And then we need to build a sled," Lana said, startling her.

"A sled? Why?"

"We need a way to get him out of here as soon as possible. We can't stay in this camp tonight. It's too dangerous."

She wondered if Vasily had told Lana about the snowmen. "It's going to be dark soon. We have no choice; we have to stay the night. But maybe we can leave first thing tomorrow, if Andrew feels strong enough."

If he were suffering from altitude sickness, decreasing their altitude should help. A sled was a good idea, though. Nat couldn't imagine him getting back to the village under his own power. Not that soon.

Steven dropped another load of branches on the pile. "What about the podcast?"

"At this point, the cast is the least of my worries. I think we should chalk this up as a failed experiment and get everyone home safe. But we can't leave without Joe and Anubha. We have to find them first."

The mountaineer nodded, but he didn't look happy. From the beginning, his enthusiasm for the investigation had outweighed Nat's own, and yet the man wasn't the type to go nuts over conspiracy theories. He was much too pragmatic. So what was in it for him? Perhaps she'd get the opportunity to ask him that night.

"Lana, you said you saw blood? Whereabouts?" Steven asked.

She lifted a quivering hand long enough to point at the woods on the opposite side of the pass.

"I'm going to check it out. Hopefully I'll be back before too long."

"I'm coming with you." Nat pushed herself to her feet before she had the chance to change her mind.

"Are you sure? Whatever we find might not be pretty."

"I'm sure. Besides, we shouldn't separate. No one should wander off unaccompanied, especially with two people missing."

"I could get Igor to go with me. Or Vasily."

"No, we need them to gather more wood and take care of the others. I'll be fine. I don't scare easily. Let's go."

When they told the others their plan, Nat braced herself for more resistance. But Andrew and Lana were too depleted to argue, and the Russian only told them to be careful. The Mansi said nothing.

Once they'd left the relative safety of the campsite for the forest, Nat regretted her insistence. Though the woods sheltered her from the bitter wind, which should have been comforting, she felt anything but comforted. Her scalp prickled, and she quickened her step, closing the distance between her and Steven.

"Do you feel that?" She was close enough to whisper in his ear.

"What?" The mountaineer spoke in a similar hushed tone, giving her the courage to express what she felt, no matter how paranoid it sounded.

"It feels like someone is watching us." Nat was tempted to whirl around, but at the same time, she had a suspicion it was better not to know.

"Probably your Canadian friends. Who else would be lurking in here? How well did you know those two, anyway?"

She bristled at the veiled accusation. "About as well as I knew any of you. But their character references and reputations were impeccable."

"Which could be easily faked."

Right. The guy was an asshole. How could she have forgotten so soon? "I do have some experience, you know. I can sift through the bullshit."

"I'm sure you can. But, whatever their reasons were, it was wrong of them to take off and leave the rest of us without a word about where they were going. And since Joe has most of our food, it's downright irresponsible."

"Maybe the food is in their tent. Did anyone search it?" She was willing to give the trappers the benefit of the doubt. They'd been hired for their hunting ability. After Vasily gave them grief about trying to do their job, it made sense they would have slipped away when he wasn't paying attention. There probably hadn't been an opportunity to let the others know. At least, that was what Nat hoped. There had to be a rational explanation.

"Not as far as I know, unless Lana did. We were too concerned with finding them. And after Joe nearly took my head off the other night, *I* certainly wasn't going anywhere near their tent."

"Understandable."

Steven whistled under his breath. "Hey, check that out."

Nat leaned forward, steadying herself on his arm to get a closer look. Snowshoe tracks. They were on the right path.

"And see the ski trail cutting across? That must be Lana's. I can't see her wandering off too far on her own. We should be close."

That's what she was afraid of. The skin on the back of her neck tightened, intense enough to make her shudder. "What do you think about what Lana said? About the blood? Do you think—"

"No. I'm thinking they killed something. It's what they do, correct?"

Praying he was right, Nat followed Steven farther into the forest, focusing on the snowshoe tracks. They were fresh, proving that Joe and Anubha had been fine not long ago.

The trees thinned, and the forest ended abruptly. Directly ahead, Nat could see the remains of a small fire under a towering cedar. Two familiar figures huddled around it, their backs to Nat and Steven.

Relief giving her renewed energy, Nat hurried forward, her mouth open to call out when Steven threw out his arm, holding her in place. He held a finger to his lips. "Don't move. Something's not right."

Then Nat saw the blood. It dotted the ground in ominous polka dots around the fire, circling to the cedar tree. Under the tree was a large, dark puddle, a stain on the snow that stretched nearly as long as the cedar's shadow.

"We have to go to them, Steven."

"I'll go. You stay here."

"What? I'm not staying here."

Steven rested his hands on her shoulders, staring at her with those unnerving eyes of his. "They're dead, Nat. Do you really want to see them like that? The only reason to go over there is to check for supplies we can use. They're gone."

"They're not dead." Nat tried to laugh, to show how ludicrous the very idea was, but it emerged as a strangled choke. "That's crazy. They're sitting right there."

"Can't you smell it?"

She hadn't, until Steven pointed it out. Death. The sweet, iron tang of blood. "It could be an animal, like you said."

"I don't think so. Wait here. If I'm wrong, you'll know in less than a minute."

Heart in her throat, Nat hugged herself as Steven crept into the clearing, studying his surroundings like a rabbit watching for a hawk. When he reached the fire, he knelt in front of the trappers. She didn't need to see the grimace on his face to know the truth. Anubha and Joe didn't move. They didn't say anything, or turn to wave at her. Either they were asleep, or...

Steven gently removed a strap from Anubha's shoulder. Nat recognized it immediately. It was Joe's backpack, the one they'd carried the food and cooking supplies in. Its existence, its very presence in that terrible place, confirmed their identities more than their clothing had. She wanted to wail as she remembered Anubha's smile, Joe's quiet confidence. How could they be gone? This had to be a nightmare, a horrible nightmare she'd soon awake from.

In spite of Steven's caution, the movement was enough to disturb Anubha's body. The woman fell backward, exposing a swollen face that was purple with bruises. Where her nose and eyes should have been were torn, bloody holes.

Nat screamed.

~ CHAPTER TEN ~

Nat trembled so violently she could barely push away the plate of spaghetti Steven offered her. Feeling her gorge rise, she covered her nose.

"No thanks. I don't want any."

"You have to eat something. I'm afraid you're going into shock. How about a little coffee spiked with Igor's finest?"

"I thought you didn't approve of drinking."

"Desperate times call for desperate measures, and these are definitely desperate times."

Nat wondered how he could be so chipper. Every time she pictured Anubha's mutilated face, she nearly lost it again. Who could have done that to her and Joe? They were such good people.

She'd wanted their bodies brought back to camp, but Steven had convinced her otherwise, fearing the smell might attract wild animals. Still, it bothered her to think of them out there alone, huddled around their dead fire. She'd make sure they got a decent burial if it was the last thing she did.

Vasily sat across from her, quietly eating his spaghetti and meatballs—the first time he'd shared a meal with the rest of the group. Maybe this tragedy would finally bring them together as a team, or perhaps the guide had just exhausted his supply of dried meat.

Nat never wanted to eat something from Joe's backpack again, no matter how hungry she was. It felt like stealing.

"I think you'd better tell us about these snowmen." Nat addressed the Mansi, careful to speak quietly, but she wasn't quiet enough.

"What are you talking about?" Steven asked. "What snowmen?"

"The ones who rule this mountain. Vasily told me about them when we first arrived at camp, and if they're the ones who murdered Joe and Anubha, they have a lot to answer for."

Lana whimpered. Thankfully, she hadn't ventured any closer to the trappers' bodies once she'd noticed the blood. She'd been spared seeing the ruin that was Anubha's face.

"Are they another tribe, Vasily?"

For a moment, Nat thought the Mansi was going to ignore Steven's question. Then he shook his head. "No, no other tribe. Not human."

"What do you mean, not human?" Cold fingers crept up Nat's spine. "No animal is capable of that. Whoever murdered them staged their bodies. They wanted us to find them that way."

"Sitting around a fire under that cedar tree. Just like Doroshenko and Krivonischenko," Steven said.

"Who are Doroshenko and Krivonischenko?" Lana asked.

"Two of the Dyatlov victims. The first two bodies the searchers found were sitting around a fire under that same tree, if I'm not mistaken. And they were both badly beaten."

"It has to be a coincidence. Doesn't it?" The Olympian's voice took on a pleading tone, and Nat hoped Steven would be gentle. However, hoping for Steven to be anything other than direct was futile.

"I don't think so. The placement of their bodies was too deliberate."

"What does that mean?" Her voice rose, and Nat could see Lana was on the verge of tears. "Are these snowmen going to pick us off one by one? And if they're not human, what are they?"

"They're abominable snowmen. Right, Vasily? You're talking about yetis," Steven said.

"That's crazy. You've both gone mad. Yetis don't exist. They're a children's story," Lana said.

Before Steven could open his mouth, Vasily slapped his hide-clad leg, as if to get their attention. "Yes, they do exist. I have seen them."

"Where, Vasily?" Igor asked. The Russian wasn't laughing. Somehow, talk of yetis seemed a little less ridiculous in the Ural Mountains, a short trek away from their colleagues' mutilated bodies. "You have seen them here?"

The Mansi poked at the fire with a stick. "No, in my village. When the winter is very, very difficult, they come to feed. Generations ago, they terrorized us. Murdered our children and destroyed our livestock. But now, we are prepared. We leave sacrifices for them. We respect them and they respect us."

"Sacrifices? Not *people?*" Lana cried.

Vasily frowned, looking at her as though she were insane. "No, not people. We are not monsters. We leave fresh meat for them. Usually yak." He paused, drawing a shaky breath. "*Many* yak. It is very difficult for my village to sacrifice so much, but it is better than letting them take what they want. We have an uneasy peace."

"And when Anubha and Joe set traps here, they broke that peace?" Steven asked.

"Yes. I tried very much to warn them, but they would not listen to me. I only hope their actions will not hurt my people."

Nat swallowed hard. She'd heard a lot of bizarre stories through her work on *Nat's Mysterious World*, and had always tried to keep an open mind. But yetis? Perhaps there was another, more human explanation.

"Couldn't they be another tribe who dresses like snow creatures in order to scare people away? Like Vikings?"

"They are bigger than any human man. Stronger, too. We have seen them crush cars, pull roofs off houses. Their voices will turn your blood to ice."

It sounded like a fairy story, albeit one written by the Brothers Grimm. "But if you knew they were here, Vasily, why did you agree to this trip? Why didn't you warn us?"

"It would be the same as the other groups. No one believes until it is too late. Besides, it has never been a problem before. No one else try to hunt here."

Steven cleared his throat. "I guess we know what happened to the Dyatlov group now."

"You don't seriously believe this, do you?" Lana asked. "Yetis are a story told to scare children. They don't actually exist."

"Perhaps you should go back to the forest and take a closer look at our friends. Tell me if you think an animal did that to them. Or a person, for that matter."

"Let us not be disrespectful to our Mansi friend. He grew up in these mountains. He has told us what he has seen. We would do well to listen to him," Igor said.

The Olympian colored. "You're right. I'm sorry, Vasily. I meant no disrespect. It's just so hard to believe."

Vasily tipped his head. "I understand. The snowmen are our reality, but they have not been yours until now. Suddenly, we have a shared problem."

Surprised Andrew had been silent for so long, Nat panicked when she saw her friend slumped over, his chin resting on his chest. Closer inspection showed his breathing was deep and even. He had fallen asleep.

"Will they let us leave? What if we made them some food?" Steven asked.

"They usually eat entire yaks. I don't think a few packets of dehydrated beef stroganoff will appease them."

"It may not satisfy them, Lana. But it might act as a peace offering, a show of good faith, especially when they see we're not hunters. What do you think, Vasily?"

The Mansi shrugged. "It is worth a try. Perhaps they feel killing the others will be enough retribution."

Steven stood up and stretched. "That's good enough for me. We have to do something, since we're obviously not going anywhere tonight."

"We might not be going anywhere tomorrow, either," Lana reminded him. "It depends on Andrew. He may need more rest."

The mountaineer paused from where he was rifling through Joe's pack. "I assume you've heard the phrase, 'survival of the fittest.'"

His words hit Nat like a slap across the face. Wrapping an arm around Andrew, she pulled her sleeping friend close. "We are *not* leaving him here to die."

"Would you have all of us die instead? Is that a better solution?"

"I will carry him down the mountain if I have to. We will leave here together," Igor said.

"Thank you." She gave the Russian a grateful smile. "Happy to see one guy who isn't a soulless prick."

"Hey, I'm not trying to be an asshole here. I'm the one trying to buy us more time. But this has turned into a matter of survival. And since it's a life-and-death situation, what you're suggesting doesn't make sense." Steven returned to the fire, tossing several packets of beef tips in gravy onto the snow.

Lana wrinkled her nose. "I'd quit while you're ahead, Steven. Nat is right. You *are* sounding like a prick, and that's a kind way of putting it."

"Look, I like Andrew. We all do. But if he can't leave, and we stay here with him, he'll still die. And the rest of us will die with him."

"You do not know that. We don't know enough about these creatures," Igor said. "I will not abandon any one of you. I would rather die with honor than live with that shame."

"Then I'll say the same to you that I said to her." Steven tipped his chin at Lana. "You need to go have a good look at what's left of Joe and Anubha."

The horrible vision of Anubha's devastated face invaded Nat's brain before she could prevent it. She pressed her hands over her ears. "Stop it. Just stop it."

"It's only fair, Nat. If they're going to volunteer to get us killed, they deserve to see what's coming. They should have *all* the information, don't you think?"

Her lip curled. "Sometimes I really hate you. I wish you'd never come on this trip."

"Someone has to tell the truth, and that role's fallen to me. I didn't choose it," he said, sounding hurt. Good to know he actually had feelings.

"There's a difference between telling the truth and being nasty, a distinction you apparently fail to grasp. Next you'll be claiming you're a realist." She really did hate people like Steven—people who only saw the worst in everyone, who infected the world around them with their gloom and doom. That was the last thing they needed up here.

He widened his eyes. "I *am* a realist. What's wrong with that?"

"You're not a realist; you're a pessimist. That's the problem. People like you never know the difference."

"And you're incredibly selfish."

Lana gasped. "Steven!"

"What? It's okay for her to insult me, but I can't say she's selfish?" He pointed at Nat, his finger stabbing the frigid air. "This is *your* expedition. For better or worse, you are supposedly leading this team, and that makes everyone's health and well-being your responsibility. Two people are dead, and we have our guide telling us that the longer we stay, the worse everyone's chances of survival are. Your priority should be saving as many lives as you can, not sacrificing everyone for your precious producer."

Nat sucked in a breath, hoping against hope Andrew was still asleep. "I'm sorry if I don't value his life less because he works for me. I wouldn't abandon you either, as disagreeable as you are."

"No one needs to be abandoned. If Igor is willing to carry Andrew with our help, what's the problem?" Lana asked. "We don't need to fight about this. We shouldn't be fighting about anything. We should be working together. And I still think we should build a sled."

At least the Olympian was thinking clearly. Steven had no clue how to survive *with* people. Nat was willing to bet the mountaineer had never lived with anyone, aside from his parents.

"The problem is, carrying him will slow us down. Igor is the strongest member of our team. Do we really want to weaken him unnecessarily? What if his strength becomes crucial to our survival? We might as well shoot ourselves in the foot before we leave. And the terrain is too steep to control a sled."

"Carrying him will not weaken me. I am stronger than that."

Nat waited, wondering if Steven would argue with the Russian about how strong he was. But even he appeared to realize that would be futile. Sighing, Steven melted snow for the packets of beef tips. "I'm done fighting with you people. I've tried my best to reason with you, but you didn't believe Vasily and now you don't believe me. Just know that if the worse comes to worst on this mountain tomorrow, you brought it on yourself."

"What do you mean, we're not listening to Vasily? We listened to Vasily." Igor's voice was angrier than Nat had ever heard it. *Uh oh.* She hoped Steven was smart enough to apologize and shut up before he got seriously hurt.

"You're listening to Vasily *now*, now that Joe and Anubha are dead. But how many people believed him when he warned us about the hunting?"

65

Igor made a scoffing sound. "I wasn't here when he talked about hunting. I was with Andrew and Nat."

"You're right." Steven raised his hands in surrender. "I'm sorry. I only meant that Anubha and Joe didn't listen, and look what happened to them. They're dead."

"Can we please stop talking about that?" Lana's voice cracked. "It's bad enough knowing their bodies are right there without you constantly bringing it up."

"Not to mention it's pretty damn close to victim blaming," Nat said, furious on her trappers' behalf. "Joe and Anubha did not deserve what happened to them. They were only doing what I paid them to do. And I'm not going to fault them if they didn't believe yetis ruled this mountain. That would be difficult for most people to wrap their heads around."

Tearing open the packets of beef tips, Steven poured them into the boiling water, making a rich gravy that got Nat's stomach growling.

"Are we really going to waste our precious food on a fabled snow creature, like some macabre version of leaving cookies for Santa?" Lana asked.

"Different cultures believe different things. The best way to survive is always to listen to the natives," Steven said, stirring the mixture. "As weird as it may sound to us, we need to listen to Vasily. He knows how to survive on this mountain, while we clearly do not."

"But we *are* listening to Vasily. We're even listening to you. I just don't want to leave Andrew—or anyone—behind." Nat studied the Mansi, who had gone quiet again. She wondered if it was a natural reticence, or the difficulty of communicating in English. "What do they look like, Vasily?" When she received a puzzled expression in return, she clarified. "The snowmen, what do they look like? Do they really have long, white fur?"

The guide shrugged. "I do not know. Never got a close look. They wear these suits, like snowsuits with hoods, but made of animal skins. Many different types of animals, different types of fur. Maybe that is how the story began that *they* are covered with fur."

Creatures wearing homemade snowsuits. Nat thought back to the story Steven had shared, about the creature in California wearing makeshift shoes. If the snowmen were capable of constructing their own clothing, they were highly intelligent. This went far beyond chimpanzees using sticks to scoop termites from a rotten log. The snowmen could be just as smart as humans, if not more so. God knows Nat had never believed their species had cornered the market on brains.

But if they couldn't outwit them and couldn't overpower them, what could they do? They didn't even have weapons beyond Anubha's crossbow, Joe's knife, and Vasily's old rifle.

"If these creatures exist, why has no one ever found a body?" Lana asked. It was an old question, one that had been put to cryptozoologists for years. Nat was curious to see if anyone in their group had an intelligent answer.

"Maybe they bury their dead. Or eat them. Or burn them," Steven said. "Or maybe bodies have been found, but the government hushed it up. We *know* something was hinky with the Dyatlov investigation. There were always too many unanswered questions. And before you jump down my throat, I'm not a conspiracy theorist. But I know, without a doubt, these creatures exist, or at least that something like them does. I've seen one."

"Even then, you'd think someone would have found something. A bit of bone, a tooth. It's almost impossible to get rid of a body entirely." Nat's obsession with true crime had told her as much. "An ordinary fire wouldn't cut it."

"Maybe people have found something, but didn't recognize it as anything extraordinary. Or maybe they were afraid. Sightings of these creatures are always in remote areas—mountains, forests. Not places where there's sophisticated technology or teams of scientists."

Steven had a point, but she could tell the others struggled with the notion that yetis were real. For many, it was much easier to believe in ghosts, vampires, and UFOs. But why?

The group fell silent for a bit, the only sound the crackling and popping of their fire. Nat tilted her head back, amazed at the brightness of the stars. This place did have a stark beauty. If only her heart weren't weighed down by fear and grief.

She thought of Lyudmila. Was this how the young skier had felt on the last night of her life? She must have known her friends were dead by the time she was killed. How had she ended up under the snow? Had the creatures buried her there?

"It's ready. Where should I put it, Vasily?" Steven poured the contents of the cooking pot onto a plate. When the savory-smelling steam hit Nat's nose, her stomach growled even louder. She pressed both hands against it.

"Over there." The Mansi pointed toward the forest, far away from their tents, filling Nat with relief. "Away from us."

"How do we know some other wild animal isn't going to come along and eat it?" Lana asked. Nat had wondered the same.

"They wouldn't dare. All creatures fear the snowmen," Vasily said. "They will leave it."

Nat wasn't sure how a fox or wolf would know whom the food was intended for, but she was too tired to ask. In spite of her hunger, her overwhelming need was for sleep. She felt dead on her feet.

"Do you think this will work? Will they leave us alone?" Igor asked.

The Mansi shrugged. "It is impossible to say. I have never seen them angry before. My village is careful to stay on their good side."

"So we have to wait and see if they're going to come kill us? Well, that's wonderful. Maybe we should make our way down to the second camp. Even in the dark, we'd probably be better off."

Nat had to agree with Lana. If there was a good chance they were going to die anyway, it made sense to leave now, while they still could.

"I cannot carry Andrew in the dark. It's too risky." Igor frowned as he looked at her producer, who was still sleeping, his head resting against her shoulder. "We'll have to wait until morning."

"What if a couple of us went ahead, like we did last night? I could go with Steven, and you three could meet us in the morning," Lana suggested.

In other words, you don't care if *we* die, Nat thought. You're only concerned about saving your own skin. She couldn't judge the woman too harshly, though. If Nat didn't have to stay behind with Andrew, she would probably already be on her way down the mountain herself. Even in the weak firelight, she could see Lana's eyes were wide with fear.

"I don't think that's a good idea." Steven had returned from placing the food at the edge of the forest. "It's better we stay together. Splitting up hasn't worked out too well for us."

Talk about the understatement of the year. If the group had remained together, would Joe and Anubha be alive? Would Nat have taken Vasily seriously enough to help convince the trappers not to hunt? It was impossible to know.

"What are we going to do?" Lana asked. "We can't lie in our tents all night, waiting to die."

"We should take turns keeping the fire going. A good, strong fire might be enough to deter them, since they attack at night. The light from it could scare them off." Steven added more kindling to the blaze. "Tending this is going to be a full-time job."

"If they're smart enough to make snowsuits, I don't think a little fire is going to scare them," Nat said. "It doesn't sound like we're dealing with primitive creatures here."

Igor cracked his knuckles. "At least it's something to do. Lana is right; we can't lie around waiting. We'll go insane."

"I volunteer to take the first shift. Lana, you should bunk with Nat and Andrew tonight. It's not safe to stay by yourself. Vasily, you can share with me and Igor," Steven said.

Nat fully expected the Mansi to refuse, but to her surprise he nodded and went to collect his sleeping bag. It would be damn crowded in their little two-person tent, but she'd feel better knowing a strong, healthy person was with them. Given Andrew's current condition, he wouldn't be of much use to her in a fight.

"I'll stay with you," Igor told Steven. "You should not be alone."

"No, you have to get your rest. We're going to need your strength tomorrow. I'll be fine. If I see anything, I'll yell my head off, I promise."

Nat gently shook Andrew by the shoulder. "Andy?" She was relieved when her producer moaned. "Andy, it's time to go to bed. Can you walk to the tent? I'll help you."

Between her and the Russian, they got Andrew to his feet. "I'm so exhausted," he said. "I can't remember feeling this tired in my life."

"All the better reason to go to bed. Come on." Hugging her friend around his waist, she was grateful for Igor's help as he supported Andrew's other side. *He's not going to be better by tomorrow.* The terrible thought flashed through her mind before she could stop it. No matter what, she would never leave Andrew behind. Was Steven right? Did that make her selfish?

Once they reached the tent, Andrew recovered enough energy to crawl inside his sleeping bag. Nat gave the Russian a hug.

"Thanks, Igor."

"No problem. I am right beside you, okay? You need anything, you yell for me and I will come."

"Okay, I will. Thank you."

It was comforting to know Igor would be close by, although if Vasily were correct about the snowmen's size and strength, it wouldn't make much difference. If the creatures were determined to destroy them, their group wouldn't stand a chance.

Leaving the flap partially open for Lana, Nat scrambled into her own sleeping bag. Remembering how the Dyatlov group had been found in their socks, she made the decision to keep her boots on, though that would make it more difficult to get in and out of the bag.

Somewhat settled, she stared into the darkness, waiting for Lana.

~ CHAPTER ELEVEN ~

Nat's eyes fluttered open. It took her a moment to remember where she was. She sat bolt upright and regretted it immediately as the blood rushed from her head, making her dizzy.

Beside her, Andrew snored softly, his breathing deep and even. His color was better, and he wasn't making that nasty wheezing sound any longer. All good signs. Still, something nagged at her. What was it?

Lana. The Olympian was supposed to have shared a tent with them, but there was no sign she'd ever arrived. The flap was partly unzipped, the way Nat had left it the night before. *Shit.*

Struggling to free herself from her sleeping bag, she tried to tell herself there were lots of innocent explanations for Lana's absence. Maybe she'd decided to stay with Steven—Nat had detected more than a few sparks between them. Or perhaps it was too crowded in here and she had decided to remain in her own tent. There was no need to panic.

Tell that to her heart, which was fluttering like a crazed bird bent on escape.

Finally yanking her boots free of the sleeping bag, Nat lifted the tent flap, wincing at the blast of wintery air. It was definitely getting colder. At least they'd be leaving today. The trick was surviving one more night on the mountain, and then they'd be back in their cozy hotel, planning the long journey home.

She could hardly wait to eat a meal that hadn't come out of a foil packet.

Igor sat beside the fire, idly stirring the embers with a stick. The flames weren't as high as they had been last night, but she could feel the warmth from a few feet away. The pile of kindling had dwindled. That would need to be the first order of business, after she made sure Lana was okay.

He grinned when he saw her approach. "Good morning."

"Good morning, Igor. Did you sleep well?"

"Shockingly, yes. I must have been more tired than I thought. How about you?"

"Too well, apparently." At his look of confusion, Nat hurried to explain. "I wanted to stay awake until Lana came in, but I must have fallen asleep. Have you seen her this morning?"

"No. Is she not in your tent?"

"It doesn't look like she ever joined us. I guess she decided to stay in hers. Can't say I blame her. It would have been very crowded with the three of us."

"Doesn't matter. We needed to stick together; that's what we decided. She should have stayed with you."

"I'm going to check on her, make sure she's okay. That's all I care about right now."

Dread loomed over Nat as she walked to the woman's tent. Next to the Mansi's, it was closest to the forest. Craning her neck, she tried to see if the plate of food Steven had left was empty, but it was too far away.

"Lana?" Nat kept her voice low, not wanting to wake Steven and Vasily if she didn't have to. "Lana, are you in there?"

There was no response, but she hadn't expected any. The Olympian had been so scared about staying alone last night. She wouldn't have done it willingly. Kneeling, Nat unzipped the tent, shaking off the feeling she was intruding. Lana had given up the right to privacy when she hadn't joined them.

Part of her, a tiny, ugly part that would always be tormented by Anubha's ruined face, had expected to find some awful scene, but Lana's tent was neat. Neat and empty, except for a note. The blonde had folded it so it stood up on its own like a place card.

This was good. Murder victims didn't have time to write letters. But where was Lana's stuff? Nat had a feeling that whatever Lana had to say, it wasn't going to make her happy. Pulling off a glove with her teeth, she unfolded the paper.

I'm sorry but I can't stay here. I've gone on to the second camp, where Nat and Igor stayed with Andrew on the first night. I'll wait there for one day, but if I don't see you, I'll continue on to Vizhai and meet you there. Forgive me.

"That stupid bitch. That stupid, selfish bitch."

"Nat?" Igor called her from right outside the tent, making her jump. "Is everything all right?"

"She left us. She fucking *left* us."

There was a rustling sound as Igor poked his head inside. "What do you mean, 'left us'?"

"See for yourself." Nat waved her arms at the empty tent before thrusting the note into the Russian's hand. "How she got past Steven is beyond me. Unless he was in on it."

Then she heard the voice of the man himself. "What's going on? What happened?" The mountaineer pulled the flap aside and stared at them, his face drawn and anxious.

"Lana left. She went to the second camp without us," Igor said, passing Steven the letter.

"You must have seen her leave," Nat said, trying and failing to keep the accusation out of her voice. "She would have had to pass you."

"Well, I didn't. Obviously. If I'd seen her, she wouldn't have gotten very far." The mountaineer scowled. "What a colossally stupid risk to take. She could have broken her neck, navigating that slope at night."

With Igor crouched beside her and Steven blocking the entrance, Nat felt claustrophobic. She pushed past the two men, grateful for the fresh air outside, even though it was freezing. They followed her out. "Maybe she left in the morning. At dawn, before I woke up and saw she was missing. She might not be too far ahead."

"That would have been Igor's shift. Did you hear or see anything?" Steven asked.

The Russian's cheeks reddened. "I might have closed my eyes for a little bit. Just a little bit. I'm sorry; I have been so tired."

Steven's jaw tightened, but before he could speak, Nat laid a hand on his arm.

"To be fair, the idea was to tend the fire, not to make sure no one escaped from camp. What's done is done. There's no point getting into a debate about whose fault this is."

"But you were more than willing for it to be mine."

Damn, did nothing get past this guy? "True, but that was more your relationship with her than anything else. I thought she might have confided in you."

"What relationship? We didn't have a relationship." Steven's eyebrows rose until they all but disappeared under his hat.

"Sorry if I misunderstood. I only meant you two were friends. She seemed to talk to you more than anyone else."

"If she did, I didn't notice. In any case, I would never have gone along with this, friend or not. If she were insistent, I would have woken everyone up and split us into groups. It's not safe for anyone to wander around out here alone. I don't care how experienced they are."

Igor stamped his feet to warm them. "So, what do we do now? Do we go after her?"

"No. It was her decision to take off. She can cool her heels for a while. Nat, I'm sorry I called you selfish yesterday. Wanting to stay with Andrew isn't selfish. *This* is selfish."

She was taken aback by the mountaineer's apology. "It's okay."

"It might be worth seeing if Vasily is willing to catch up with her after breakfast, but I'm still of a mind that we shouldn't separate any more than we already have. Vasily is our guide, the one who knows the most about these mountains. If something happens to him—"

Nat shivered. "Don't even think it."

"And we have Andrew's condition to consider," Steven continued. "Is he awake?"

"He wasn't when I got up, but he was looking a lot better. His breathing sounded better too."

"Good." He clapped her on the shoulder. "See, things are looking up. She should have waited. Why don't I make some breakfast, and we'll see how everyone feels once we've eaten?"

"Sounds like a plan. Did you check the plate?" Though Nat wasn't sure she believed in the snowmen, she couldn't help being curious.

"Not yet. I'll do that right now. Igor, can you gather some firewood? I'll need a bit more heat if I'm going to cook."

"Yah, sure."

Nat followed the Russian into the brush. It was better than sitting at the fire alone. Her nerves were on edge. First Anubha and Joe, and now Lana. What was with people taking off? She was beginning to think Steven might end up being the best team player they had, and how scary was that?

"Sorry, Nat."

"For what?" Meeting the Russian's eyes, she was surprised to see how miserable he looked, like his dog had died.

"For falling asleep. I should have been awake. I should have caught her."

"It's not your fault. None of us signed up for this, and we're all running on empty. It could have happened to anyone. Besides, even if you had caught her, there's not much you could have done."

"I could have held her down until you woke up." His mouth curved in a half smile.

"Maybe, but at the end of the day, we're all adults. If she was determined to leave, we wouldn't have any right to stop her. What if something had happened to us in the night, and by leaving, she was the only survivor? I'm sure she thought she was doing the right thing."

Nat hoped she sounded more convincing than she felt. In truth, she could have cheerfully strangled the woman. Lana was the one who'd known the most about altitude sickness. How were they supposed to monitor Andrew's condition without her?

"I feel bad. I think I could have talked her out of it," Igor said.

"Try not to worry about it. We'll meet up with her soon enough."

Their arms full of branches and twigs, they made their way back to the fire where Steven waited. The mountaineer held up an empty plate as they approached. "Check it out. It's been licked clean. I think the peace offering worked."

"Assuming the snowmen took it, yah," Igor said, kneeling to pile new sticks on the fire.

"We're alive, aren't we? I'd call that an unqualified success."

"Vasily's okay?" Nat realized she hadn't seen the Mansi yet.

"Alive and well. He went into the bush to take care of some business, if you know what I mean." Steven grinned.

Nat wrinkled her nose. "Enough said. I guess I should wake Andrew."

"You can, or you can wait until breakfast's ready." Scanning the directions on the pack of breakfast burritos, Steven stretched his neck with a groan. "Should take about fifteen minutes."

"In that case, I should start now. He's a slow riser."

Which was true, but more importantly, Nat was eager to share the news about Lana. Maybe Andrew would have a better idea of what they should do.

When she entered the tent, her friend was already awake, staring at the ceiling.

"Well, look who's up. Good morning."

He didn't answer. It was as though she hadn't said a word. She moved closer, shuffling on her knees until she was beside him. "Andrew? What's wrong? Do you feel sick?"

"I knew I recognized his voice. It was so familiar. I *knew* I'd heard it before. I just couldn't place it."

The feeling of dread returned with a vengeance. Had Andrew lost his mind? Was that a symptom of altitude sickness? She seemed to recall reading that people who had it couldn't think clearly. "What are you talking about?"

He focused on her then, as if seeing her for the first time. "I'm sorry, Nat. I should have figured it out sooner."

"Figured out what? Andrew, you're scaring me."

"Everything okay in there?" Steven called from the fire.

"Everything's fine," Nat yelled back. She touched her friend's cheek, willing him to look at her again. "It *is* fine, isn't it?"

"Nat, does his voice sound at all familiar?" Andrew whispered, his words a harsh rasp.

"Who, Steven's? Not really." But that wasn't exactly true. She remembered that first night at the restaurant in Vizhai, how she'd felt like she'd met him before. "Why?"

"Something about him has always bugged me. Well, besides the obvious. And I finally realized what it was this morning, lying here, listening to him talk."

"What is it? Did you meet him somewhere?" It didn't make sense. If they'd had a prior connection to Steven, why wouldn't he have mentioned it during his interview? Surely it would have improved his chances of getting on the team.

"Not in person, no. But I've talked to him, and so have you."

"I'm sorry, but I have no idea what you're getting at. Spit it out, before they send a search party after us."

"Don't you get it? Steven is Cliff. He's the troll who's been tormenting you for months."

~ CHAPTER TWELVE ~

There was no point asking if Andrew was sure. The man had phenomenal recall when it came to names, faces, and voices. Steven was lucky her producer hadn't found him out earlier.

The question was, what did they do about it? If he really was related to Lyudmila, he had a vested interest, but that didn't necessarily mean he'd want to sabotage the trip. The opposite might be true. He *had* swallowed Vasily's yeti stories a bit too quickly, though, even if he had seen a cryptid in California. She'd expected more skepticism, especially from him.

Should she confront him? Andrew had argued against it, saying as long as they kept Cliff/Steven in the dark, they had the power. But it wouldn't be easy to hide her anger. If it hadn't been for the guy's constant baiting and heckling, she never would have gone forward with this trip. Okay, her stupid ego had had a bit to do with it too. Now two people were dead and a third had deserted them. It was all she could do to refrain from clawing his pretty blue eyes out. Let's see how alarmingly intense his gaze was without them.

"The food's almost ready. Is Andrew coming?" Steven smiled at her, completely guileless. He had no idea they knew. No clue what was coming. And there was something rather satisfying about that.

"He's not feeling up to it. I told him I'd bring him something later." In reality, Andrew didn't feel he could look Steven in the eye just yet.

"That's not good. Is he going to be able to ski today?" Steven's forehead creased in concern, and Nat wondered how much he actually cared. After all, he'd wanted to abandon Andrew from the beginning. Maybe he'd been afraid the producer would eventually figure him out.

"I'm not sure. I didn't ask him yet. But Igor, you're still okay to help, right?" After the bombshell Andrew had dropped, leaving had been the last thing on her mind. She hadn't even thought to ask him how he was feeling. *Shit.*

"Yah, I'll carry him to Vizhai if I have to. We need to leave today," the Russian said.

Nat waited for Steven to argue, to talk about the importance of everyone getting down the mountain under their own steam, but he didn't say a word. Perhaps he was finally learning.

"It's a shame we're leaving without being any closer to solving the Dyatlov mystery, though. I was really hoping we'd find out what happened to Lyudmila especially." She watched Steven out of the corner of her eye, wondering if he'd take the bait. She didn't have to wonder long.

"Why Lyudmila?"

"I don't know. I suppose I've always felt the sorriest for her. She was one of the youngest, and the most horribly injured. I'd hoped, at the very least, to be able to give her family some sort of closure. But I guess that ship has sailed."

"What are you talking about? Vasily's story confirms what happened to them."

Nat snorted, deciding to lay it on just thick enough to bait him. "That ridiculous yeti theory?" She was glad the Mansi hadn't returned from his business yet. She'd be much more reluctant to disparage his account with him sitting right there. "I'm not buying it."

"You saw Anubha and Joe. They didn't die of natural causes. How else do you explain what happened to them?"

"I actually *didn't* see them. Not close up. But the fact they're dead doesn't mean yetis killed them. Occam's razor, right? The simplest explanation is usually the truth."

Steven leaned back on his heels and stared at her, breakfast temporarily forgotten. "What are you saying? Who else could have possibly done it? No one is here but us."

"We don't know that for sure. There *could* be someone else here. If the government murdered the Dyatlov group for seeing something they shouldn't, maybe whatever it was is still here. The military could have continued to monitor it. But I agree it's unlikely."

The mountaineer's face darkened. "I repeat—what are you saying?"

"When Anubha and Joe disappeared, only you, Lana, and Vasily had the opportunity. Me, Igor, and Andrew were too far away, not to mention Andrew was in no condition to walk, let alone harm anyone. So, the killer had to have been one of you." Nat prayed he would give her some reason it couldn't be true, some indisputable proof of his innocence. As unlikeable as he had been, she couldn't see Steven as a murderer.

Then again, people had thought Ted Bundy was a real nice guy too.

"You can't seriously believe one of us was responsible. Or even capable of slaughtering them like that."

Forcing aside the horrific image of Anubha's face, Nat folded her arms across her chest. "I find that a lot more believable than some farfetched story about a tribe of yetis."

To her surprise, Igor spoke up. "Yah, Steven. The yeti story, it's a bit crazy, no?"

"You think it's more plausible that *I* killed them? For starters, Joe would have ripped me apart. For another, I don't have a motive. They were the only people capable of getting us food that doesn't come in a

77

packet. If I were going to kill anyone, it would be someone useless. Someone like—"

Nat's jaw tightened. "Don't say it. If you thought Joe could tear you apart, you don't even want to *think* what you were about to say."

Before the mountaineer could respond, someone called his name. *Screamed* it.

"Steven, Steven! You must come. Please help."

Vasily ran toward them, repeatedly losing his footing in the deep snow. His breathing ragged, the Mansi stumbled into Steven's arms, tears running down his cheeks. "You must help. Please."

All evidence of his anger gone, the mountaineer steadied the older man and spoke to him almost tenderly. "What is it? What's wrong?"

"It is the fair-haired one. She is…it is not good." His face set in lines of desperation and grief, Vasily turned to Igor and spoke rapidly, his words tumbling over each other as if in a frantic rush to escape.

Igor shook his head, lifting his hands palms up. "I'm sorry. I do not understand."

The nagging feeling something was terribly wrong returned, if it had ever really gone away. "Is he talking about Lana? But Lana left for the other site, didn't she?" Fear and helplessness became rage as Nat stared at the guide, who babbled away in a language none of them understood. Could one even call him a guide? He'd been next to useless so far. He certainly hadn't protected them. "What did you do to her? *Answer* me."

She would have shaken the truth out of him if Steven hadn't stepped between them. "Oh, so now Vasily is guilty too? You'd better get your villains straight."

"I know who my villain is…*Cliff.*"

Fuck. She hadn't meant for the name to slip out in the heat of the moment, but she'd felt too furious, too betrayed, to keep her big mouth shut. So much for retaining the power. Sorry, Andrew. She always had been lousy at keeping secrets. Didn't her producer know better than to entrust her with something like this?

Steven's face contorted as though he were in pain. "We can talk about this later."

"Why did she call you Cliff? I don't understand." Poor Igor. Between Vasily's dialect and this new drama, he looked beyond confused.

"I'll explain later. Vasily, are you talking about Lana?" At the man's blank expression, Steven raised his arm to a level slightly above his head. "Tall, blonde, pretty?"

The Mansi nodded. "Yes, yes. Please help."

"What's wrong with her?"

In response, Vasily pulled at Steven's jacket sleeves violently enough that the mountaineer slid forward. "Come, you see. Please, I have no words."

As Igor and Nat prepared to follow, the Mansi held out his hand. "No, only him. Only him see."

"I'm in charge of this expedition. If something is wrong with a member of my team, I should see it for myself."

"Please, Nat. Let me go with him, and if it's something you need to be involved in, I promise I'll tell you." Steven's face flushed as he met her eyes. "I realize it's difficult for you to trust me right now, but I swear I'm not the enemy. Though it probably seems that way."

"Look, I don't need either of you to protect me, and I don't appreciate being treated like a child. Everyone on this team is *my* responsibility, not yours, and not Vasily's. So you can either come along and keep your mouth shut, or stay here with Andrew."

Steven sized her up for a moment before shrugging. "Whatever you say. Go ahead, Vasily. Show us what you found."

Lana lay on the path between their campsite and Anubha and Joe's final resting place. Her legs were folded toward her chest, as if she'd been trying for the fetal position but couldn't quite muster the energy. Her hands covered her breasts and were clenched into fists. Her eyes were closed as though she were sleeping, but the condition of her face belied that faux peacefulness.

Her once-lovely features were swollen and dark with bruises. Deep purple and reddish abrasions covered her hands as well. Lana had not gone quietly.

Nat swallowed hard against the discomfort of déjà vu. She had seen this scene before, and she knew exactly where. By either happenstance or design, Lana's body mimicked that of Zinaida Alekseevna Kolmogorova, one of the Dyatlov group.

Eyeing the men who stood with her, heads bowed, Nat had the uncomfortable realization she was the only woman left. Lyudmila had no doubt suffered, watching her female friends die, and now she was in the same position. Given what had happened to Lyudmila, it wasn't a comforting thought.

"How could you?" The words erupted from her lips before she could think better of them. She felt Andrew's absence like a missing limb. He had always stepped in on her behalf, smoothed things over, played the diplomat. He'd saved her from herself.

Steven's brows knitted together, his features a gathering storm. For the first time, she wondered if it was smart to openly challenge this man.

If she truly believed he'd murdered three people with no motive at all, it wasn't the brightest move to give him an ironclad one.

But when he spoke, his voice didn't hint at the fury in his eyes. "You can't be serious. You can't seriously think I'm responsible for this."

"If not you or Vasily, who else?" When she said the Mansi's name, Vasily shrank back as though she'd slapped him. She watched herself as if from afar. Why was she acting this way? And worse, why couldn't she stop?

"Jesus Christ, Nat. Look at her. *Look* at her. See her hands? Whatever did this got the fight of its life. The killer would be covered in cuts and scratches, bruises for sure." Steven tilted his head, lifting his chiseled cheekbone to the light. "Take a look. Not a scratch. How do you explain that?"

"I don't know." She held her hands tightly together to keep from punching him right on his pristine chin. "I don't know, okay? I just know one of you had to have done it."

"Why? Nat, that's crazy. I could see you maybe thinking that about Joe after the scuffle we had, but what reason could I possibly have for hurting Lana? As you so discreetly pointed out, I was more than a little fond of her."

Fond of her. Unable to stand it any longer, Nat sank to her knees in the snow beside the skier's body. Taking off one of her gloves, she touched Lana's bare fist. It was cold and hard, like rock. Already frozen. The Olympian had been here a while.

"What are you doing?" Steven lifted her under the arms, pulling her to her feet, a lot more gently than she deserved, in light of the fact she'd just accused him of murder—again. "You can't touch her. There'll be evidence on her hands: skin, hair, clothing fibers, DNA. Like it or not, this is a crime scene now. The more we touch it, the more we contaminate it. We should find some plastic bags and put them on her hands, preserve the evidence as best we can."

"I'm s-sorry. You're right. She just looks so sad, so alone. I...needed to do something to comfort her."

"She's dead, Nat. The best thing we can do for her now is help the police find her killer."

"I will go find the bags," Igor said, the first words he'd spoken since Steven and Vasily had led them to the body. He'd gotten along well with Lana too. Nat remembered them laughing and joking together, the easy camaraderie they'd had. Then again, Lana had been like that with everyone. The campsite already seemed colder and more dismal without her.

"In the front pocket of my pack there are some sterile ones. We can use those," Steven said.

The Russian nodded, looking relieved to have a reason to leave, if only for a few minutes. If this continued, these woods would soon be an abattoir. Some podcaster of the future would cover the killings, talking about the great mystery of their deaths. The McPherson Pass incident. It would have been amusing if it weren't so fucking depressing.

Nat raised an eyebrow. "You brought sterile bags?" Had he been expecting a crime scene?

"Food storage. You should go with him."

"Why? I'm sure he's more than capable of finding the bags on his own."

"There's no reason for you to hang around here. You too, Vasily. Get back to the fire where it's warm. Once Igor comes back, it'll only take me a few minutes to bag her hands, and then I'll join you. We can discuss our options then."

Discuss our options. It sounded so formal, as if they were project managers at a job site instead of three dazed and deluded fools standing over the corpse of their dead friend. Nat averted her eyes. She felt guilty for not looking at Lana, but the sight of her battered body made Nat's heart twist in despair. She would forever see the woman's bruised face in her nightmares.

"Do you have experience with this sort of thing?"

Steven was too cool, too controlled. Perhaps it was an act, but it wasn't normal. Then again, nothing about this situation was normal. Any minute, Nat expected someone to lose their mind and run around the campsite yelling gibberish. Most of the time, she expected it to be her.

The corners of his mouth rose in a faint imitation of a smirk. "Only what I've learned on CSI. Go on, Vasily. You take her back."

"I can go by myself," she protested, but the truth was, it did feel comforting when the Mansi slipped his arm through hers. The gesture was unexpected. This must have been difficult for him too. She was sure he didn't ordinarily lose three members of his group to murder.

The walk back to the campsite and their fire went much faster than their journey into the woods. Once the terrible scene was at their backs, Nat felt a desperate need to escape. She quickened her step, and Vasily, perhaps feeling the same, did as well.

She'd expected to bump into Igor on the way, and as they drew nearer and nearer to camp, an awful realization dawned on her. Once again, they'd separated. What if something had happened to the Russian? What if he were dead too? She nearly wept with relief when they made it to the clearing and she spotted him, crouched at the entrance of Steven's tent, the mountaineer's backpack in his hands.

"What's wrong? Can't you find the bags?"

Bright bursts of color flared on Igor's cheeks, and when he looked up at her, his eyes were glassy.

"What is it, Igor?"

"I found them. But I also found this." He pulled out a knife, its blade winking cruelly in the gray light. Nat was no expert on knives, but she was pretty sure it had belonged to Joe, the same blade the trapper had threatened Steven with.

Its edge was darkened with dried blood.

~ CHAPTER THIRTEEN ~

Nat clutched her head with both hands, attempting to distract herself from the pounding in her brain. It felt like they'd been fighting, hollering at each other for hours, though it had probably only been about thirty minutes. Thirty minutes of hell.

"Sue me because I thought it was smart to have some kind of weapon." Steven's voice cut through the campsite, creating an echo. It was eerie to hear his words float back to them. "Call me crazy, but as two of us were dead at that point, I thought it might be a good fucking idea to be able to defend myself."

"What is wrong with you people? Steven is not a murderer. He was right to take the knife." Vasily positioned himself between Igor and the mountaineer, as though he thought Steven were in danger of attack. Since when had he developed such a loyalty to that wretched man? Nat guessed it must have been when they were skiing so far ahead of the others.

"You have to admit it looks bad. Whose blood is on it, Steven? You still haven't answered that question," Igor said, his voice dangerously calm.

Steven threw his hands in the air. "I don't fucking know, okay? It's not like I was thinking straight. I saw it in Joe's hand and I took it. It could be yeti blood, for all I know."

"Would you stop it with the fucking yetis?" It was the third time Igor had made the same request, but the first time he'd added an f-bomb. "There's no such thing."

"Yes, there is!" Vasily's voice bordered on an indignant shriek. "I have seen them. I *told* you. I told you what happened to my village."

"You saw some big men in snowsuits. You don't know what they were. They could have been a rival tribe."

Yes. Go, Igor. At least Steven hadn't blamed the presence of the knife in his pack on a snowman. And where was Anubha's crossbow? Did he have that as well? It wasn't a comforting thought.

"They were *not* men," Vasily said, all but stomping in the snow; he was so infuriated, and Nat wondered how she ever could have thought he was a cold fish. "They are too strong! Too big."

"I do not like him having a knife. Too much death has happened when you two were here. We will not feel safe if Steven has the weapon." Igor held out his hand while Nat held her breath. What if the mountaineer snapped and stabbed him with it?

"His name is Cliff," she said, trying not to moan at the pain in her head.

"Actually, it's Steven. Cliff was a name I used for the show. Obviously, I couldn't use my real one."

"Obviously."

"What are you two talking about? I thought we were talking about the knife." Igor scowled. Since no one was currently questioning the existence of yetis, Vasily had fallen silent again. It appeared to be the only dog he had in this fight.

"I'm not sure if Steven is a murderer, but he's the reason we're in this mess." Nat sighed. "About a year ago, someone named Cliff started trolling my show."

"Trolling?" the Russian asked.

"Sorry. It's a Western expression. Basically, making our lives miserable. Calling me out for being a coward, saying I hadn't done anything noteworthy in far too long. He wanted me to investigate the Dyatlov Pass incident, and he wouldn't let up. Somehow, the bastard got under my skin. He hit me where it hurt—my overdeveloped ego. And so here we are." She stared Steven down, daring him to argue with her, but the man kept his mouth shut for a change. Hallelujah.

"That was *you*?" Igor gawked at the mountaineer. "But why?"

Steven sighed. "Because my great-aunt was Lyudmila Dubinina."

"Am I supposed to know who this is?" The Russian glanced at Nat, but it was Steven who answered.

"She was a member of the Dyatlov group. One of the youngest, and arguably the most injured. She might have also been the last to die. I learned about her death as a child, and it's haunted me ever since. I was trying to get Nat's help investigating what happened to her. Admittedly, I didn't go about it the right way."

"Didn't go about it the right way? You *terrorized* us." Talk about turning understatement into an art form.

"I'm sorry. That was never my intention. Riling you up seemed like it would be more effective than asking nicely, and you have to admit it was."

She would have loved to wipe that smug expression off his face. "Difficult to say, since you never asked nicely. You were a douche from day one."

"Granted. I'll accept that. But I'm not a murderer. And I never tried to sabotage this trip. When you were at your angriest with me, I was actually trying to help."

"I still think it's a good idea to give the knife to Igor. Or to me. If something else happens, you'll be in the clear," Nat said.

The Russian lowered his voice to a growl. "Nothing else better happen. No more. Everyone leave, we get off this Dead Mountain alive, yah."

Everyone leave. Shit, how long had it been since she'd checked on Andrew? "I should see how Andy's doing. I'll be right back." She paused for a moment, long enough to size up the man who had made her life a living hell for a year. Steven's shoulders were slumped, and he stared at his boots, moving a small hill of snow back and forth with his feet. At least the fight seemed to have gone out of him. "Steven? Please do the right thing. Give the knife to Igor. And the crossbow as well, if you have it."

Trepidation weighed on her as she rushed to the tent she shared with Andrew. *Fuck.* What if something had happened to him? How could she have stayed away so long?

It was a relief to find everything as she'd left it, with the flaps securely zipped and fastened. There'd been a small, evil part of her mind that had been scared she'd find a huge rip in the side, like the one the Dyatlov group had cut in their tent.

Andrew was on his back, fast asleep. *Thank God, thank God.* If anything had happened to him, she'd never have forgiven herself. A tiny cry escaped her and Andrew shifted in his sleeping bag, his eyes flickering open. "Nat?"

"Yeah." She pressed her hand to his forehead like a mother searching for signs of fever. His skin was warm and damp, but she didn't see any reason for alarm. "How are you feeling?"

"Tired. Cold."

"You should come and sit by the fire. That'll warm you up in a hurry." Assuming everyone stopped arguing long enough to tend it. Worse came to worst, she'd do it herself. She wasn't as good at it as Igor, but there was only one way to learn.

Andrew yawned. "What time is it? It seemed like you were gone for a really long time."

"I probably was. I'm so sorry. I never should have left you alone for that long." Nat's hand went for her phone until she remembered she'd purchased a cheap watch for the trip to keep from draining her battery. She was shocked to see it was a few minutes shy of three p.m. The sun would set in a couple of hours, making it too dangerous to leave. Assuming they *could* leave. "How are your lungs feeling? Are you out of breath?"

He took a few exaggerated breaths. The faint whistling she'd heard over the last forty-eight hours was gone. "See? I'm fine; let's go."

"It's not that easy. We'd have to pack up camp, and that takes time. Also, you haven't eaten since last night. Don't even think about attempting the descent without something in your stomach."

"Yes, mom." He rolled his eyes.

"Well, someone has to mother you, before you run out of here without your boots on." Nat caught what she'd said and winced. A few members of the Dyatlov group had been found in their socks. "Sorry."

He patted her leg. "It's okay. I knew what you meant. Can you ask Lana to come here and take a look at me? She seems to be an expert about this altitude stuff."

At the sound of Lana's name, Nat's throat closed. How on earth would she break the news? The amiable blonde hadn't just been his friend, but also the closest thing he had to a doctor out here. Not that it had kept her from abandoning him, Nat thought with a twist of bitterness, immediately followed by guilt. Lana had been terrified of her own death. She'd done what she'd felt was the right thing to ensure her survival. Too bad it had gone so horribly wrong.

Hell, for all Nat knew, Lana might not have written the note in her tent. Steven could have written it to cover his tracks.

She'd never been able to keep anything from Andrew. "What is it?" Eyes widening, he propped himself up on his elbows. "Please don't tell me she's..."

Not trusting herself to speak, Nat nodded. Safe in the security of their friendship, the tears she'd been holding back since the gruesome discovery began to fall.

"Fuck. Oh, fuck. No! What happened to her?"

Craving comfort, she lowered herself beside him, resting her head on his shoulder. "I don't know. She was pretty bruised, and her hands were frozen into fists, like she died fighting. Her body was posed, just like Anubha and Joe's."

"To recreate another Dyatlov victim?"

"Yeah. Zinaida. And whoever killed her did a much better job this time." She bit back a sob. "Oh, Andrew, it's been awful. I don't know who to trust, who to believe. Is it one of us who's doing this? I can't imagine why, but if not us, who else? And Igor found Joe's knife in Steven's bag, and it's covered in blood. I don't know if I can deal with this anymore."

"Hey. *Hey.*" He lifted his shoulder so her head rolled slightly. "You can and you will. You have no choice. You have to get us out of here. You're the only one who can."

"What are you talking about? Vasily is the guide. I can barely keep up."

"Vasily's the guide, but you're the leader. You can't give up. These people are counting on you to see them safely home. *I'm* counting on you. You can break down when we're off this godforsaken mountain, but not before. All right?"

"But how am I supposed to keep everyone safe when someone in our group is a serial killer?" She lowered her voice to a whisper. "Igor was with us at the other camp when Joe and Anubha died, so that lets him off the hook. The two of us are obviously above suspicion…"

"Clearly."

"That leaves Steven and Vasily."

"*Vasily* is a suspect now?"

"I don't know, Andrew. Like I said, I can't trust anyone."

"I honestly can't see either of them doing it. Plus, if they'd taken on Lana, they'd be marked up."

"That's what Steven said. But I'm not comfortable placing my trust in him."

"Do you really think he did it? He's a bit of a douchebag, but that doesn't mean he's a killer."

She ran the possibility over in her mind. The Ted Bundy School of False First Impressions aside, she thought it unlikely. And the mountaineer was right—he had no motive. That she knew of. But since she hadn't known he was Cliff until Andrew had told her, anything was possible. Perhaps there had been more conflict bubbling underneath the surface, conflict she wasn't aware of. Nat pictured Joe's ferocity the evening he'd lunged at Steven with his filleting knife. It had been so out of character for the soft-spoken trapper. And bizarre that he would have blamed the mountaineer instead of the most likely culprit, a wild animal.

But what if there were a history, something hidden that had passed between them? Then Joe's seemingly over-the-top reaction might be more understandable. Nat wished she had thought to ask him while she'd still had the chance.

"No, but if he didn't do it, then who else? Vasily? I can't see it."

"Maybe Vasily wants to scare the tourists away from Dead Mountain."

"Maybe." Nat remembered the gaunt face of the guide when she'd first met him, the tears in his eyes as he'd thanked her for the work, saying that now he'd be able to provide for his family. Before today, it was the last time she'd seen him emote more than your average turnip. Why would he destroy his sole source of income? The remainder of the winter promised to be long and brutal.

Unless again, there was something she didn't know, some crucial bit of information being withheld from her.

"Steven could be so obsessed with what happened to his aunt that he's recreating those crime scenes, whether consciously or subconsciously," she said.

"We're not living in a Hollywood production, Nat. Don't you think that's a tad far fetched?"

"Hey, everything okay in there?"

It was Steven. Why the hell couldn't he leave them alone?

"Yes, we're fine," Andrew called, and before they could move, Steven poked his head inside the tent. Nat pushed herself away from Andrew and sat up. She wasn't ashamed of cuddling with him, but that didn't mean she was comfortable with anyone else seeing it. But she was too late. She saw the look of shock that flitted over the mountaineer's face before he regained composure.

"Sorry, I didn't mean to interrupt."

"You're not interrupting anything." She hated the snarl in her voice. If anything, it made her appear guiltier. "We were just talking."

He glanced at Andrew and back to her, his uncertainty clear. "Can I come in and talk to you both for a sec?"

Andrew said sure before she could say the few choice words that were on her mind. Probably for the best. Steven ducked to slip inside, while Nat shuffled as far away from him as she could, until she was sitting behind Andrew's head. The mountaineer's face fell.

"Nat, I swear I didn't hurt anyone. I won't hurt you, either. I kept the knife and crossbow with me for protection, but I've done what you asked and given them both to Igor."

"Okay."

Steven turned to Andrew. "How are you feeling? Any better?"

"A little. Still pretty weak."

"That's probably because you haven't had anything to eat today. Sorry. In light of recent events, breakfast got a bit...derailed." He lifted his eyes to Nat's. "I assume you told him."

"Yes, I did." What was it about this guy that a simple question felt like an attack? She felt sick to her stomach.

"We need to get out of here. Before anyone else dies." The resolve in Andrew's words was impressive, considering that, as far as Nat knew, he hadn't stood up yet that day.

"I agree, but even now we're losing daylight."

Nat's spirits plummeted even further. She hadn't noticed the shadows lengthening, but Steven was right. Soon it would once again be too dark to leave.

"I don't care," Andrew said. "I'll risk a broken leg over lying here like a lamb waiting for slaughter."

"I get what you're saying, I do, but you'll suffer a lot more than a broken leg if you fall off the side of this mountain."

"At least it would be a quick end."

"Don't say that, Andy. We have to be smart about this."

"Nat's right. Why don't you both come over to the fire, and we'll figure out the next course of action. Vasily wants to leave too. Perhaps he knows a safe way of navigating this place at night."

The idea of stumbling around in the dark, with who knows what behind them or in front of them, made her shudder. But how could she possibly spend another night at the campsite? It was becoming a graveyard.

"I want to apologize for the whole trolling thing. It wasn't the right way to go about it, and I'm sorry if my actions eroded any trust you might have had in me." Steven took off his cap, running a hand through his dark hair. "I've been trying to get someone to investigate my great-aunt's death for years, without any luck, and I'd listened to *Nat's Mysterious World* long enough to know Nat didn't back away from a dare. I thought it was worth a shot, but I now see that it was wrong, and I'm sorry."

"Why didn't you go on your own? It's not like you needed any of us." She refused to accept his apology. He'd made her life a living hell, and now he was at least indirectly responsible for three deaths. He didn't deserve to be forgiven.

"I didn't have the experience with this sort of thing, the budget, or the equipment. Sure, I probably could have made it to Vizhai and hired my own guide, but then I wouldn't have proper witnesses, either. And after what I saw in California, I wanted to make sure I did this time."

"Honestly? I think you're only sorry you got caught. You kept the Cliff thing going for over a year. If you felt at all remorseful about it, there were plenty of opportunities to redeem yourself, but no. You antagonized us because you got off on it." Nat's jaw clicked and she realized she'd been clenching her teeth. She had to calm down before she slugged the guy.

"You do seem to enjoy provoking people, judging by how you've behaved on this trip," Andrew added.

"I never mean to. It's a character flaw. I rub people the wrong way."

"I'm sorry, but that's a cop-out. That makes it sound like it's an accident. You *deliberately* sniped at everyone, every chance you got. And don't think I didn't hear you arguing to leave me behind." As Andrew glowered at Steven, Nat wanted to cheer. It was about time someone other than her dressed this guy down. He'd been a thorn in their side from the beginning.

"That wasn't very compassionate of me, I admit. But I was only thinking of what was best for the group as a whole."

At his attempt to portray himself as altruistic, Nat lost it. "Bullshit. Since when have you cared about the group? If you really wanted to find out what happened to your aunt, there's no way you'd want to leave now. These murders are obviously recreations of what happened in 1959. The longer we stay, the closer you get to finding the truth."

"Sure, I'd love to find out what happened to my aunt, but I'm not suicidal. In spite of my fears, I had no idea any of us were at risk, not really. Once Joe and Anubha died, it wasn't worth it anymore."

"How do we know you're not doing this yourself? You admit you're obsessed with the case. You're the only one, other than Vasily, who had the opportunity to kill Joe, Anubha, and Lana." Andrew's voice broke when he said Lana's name, and tears welled in Nat's own eyes. "You're the only one with a motive."

Steven raised an eyebrow. "Are you serious? I want to find out what happened to my aunt, and that's enough of a motive to murder three people? You can't actually believe that."

"Maybe your aunt's death isn't the motive. Maybe you killed Joe and Anubha because of your run-in with them the other night," Nat said. "Lana could have spurned your advances."

"Trust me, there were no 'advances,' and if there had been, she wouldn't have spurned them."

"You conceited asshole." She'd never wanted to strangle someone so much in her life.

"I'm not being conceited. Like you mentioned, we were fond of each other. But she lived in Canada; I'm in California. What would have been the point of starting anything?"

"I'd like to think she had better taste."

Steven winced. "Ouch. Hey, I get you're both pissed at me, and I don't blame you. I probably deserve everything you can throw at me—"

"Probably?" Andrew asked.

"Okay, I *definitely* deserve it. But I came in here to make peace, to see if there's some way we can get past this. Let's not forget that something out there is picking us off one by one, and this is what it wants. The more we turn on each other, the easier it will be for them to eliminate us."

Andrew rolled his eyes. "Them? You're not still pretending you believe this yeti theory, are you?"

"Here. I want to show you something." Reaching into the inside pocket of his jacket, the mountaineer withdrew a folded sheet of paper and handed it to Nat. It was a copy of a photograph, a famous photograph she'd seen before, the one that had been found in the camera in Dyatlov's tent. This version had been enhanced, which hadn't helped much. It still looked like a man in a snowsuit in the cedar forest. All the enhancement had accomplished was reveal a bit more detail in the clothing. It remained fairly fuzzy. "Check out the material of his suit. Doesn't it look like it could be hide, like Vasily described?"

Nat peered at the picture before handing it to Andrew. "Maybe. But I don't see what that has to do with anything. It could have been a member of their group, or another tribe—anything."

"If that doesn't convince you, how about this?" Steven passed Nat his phone. On the display was a close-cropped photo of a bruised hand, the fingers curled into a fist. Her stomach lurched.

"This isn't funny."

"I don't mean for it to be. Look between her fingers, Nat."

Swallowing hard over the lump that had formed in her throat, Nat examined the photo closely. It took a few seconds, but finally she saw what Steven had been getting at. Lana clutched a small piece of animal fur. It looked like part of a pelt. Or, perhaps, a homemade snowsuit.

"That doesn't prove anything. It could even mean an animal attacked her," Nat said.

"Except there were no tracks. No bite marks. And aside from the bruising, her body was in perfect condition. What kind of animal would do that?"

"I hate to interrupt this argument, but while you two are bickering, we're losing daylight. Something killed Joe, Anubha, and Lana, and I think we can all agree that we need to get the fuck out of here while we can."

Before either of them could respond to Andrew, a shadow loomed over the tent, making Nat jump.

"Hello, guys? We have a problem."

She sighed. Great. What else was new? There had been nothing but problems on this trip. Pushing past Steven, she pulled the flap aside. "What is it, Igor?"

The Russian's eyes were red and raw, as though he had been crying. "Our skis are missing. While we were with Lana, someone must have taken them."

~ CHAPTER FOURTEEN ~

It was a much-diminished group that gathered around the fire that evening, staring gloomily into the flames while the skies darkened.

And then there were five.

"We'll have to walk down, yah?" Igor kicked at a stray ember, which fizzled in the snow. The temperature had dropped dramatically, and even near the blaze it was uncomfortably cold.

"We can't. The snow is too deep in places, and it will take us too long. And what if there's a storm? We'd die," Steven said.

"We'll die for sure if we stay here." Andrew sounded so resigned Nat worried he'd lost the will to live. While his coloring and breathing had improved, and his mind appeared as sharp as ever, his spirit was lacking. And he probably needed that to survive more than anything.

"We'll die if we get trapped on the side of the mountain in a blizzard too." As usual, the mountaineer was brimming with optimism.

"Look, we all know this situation sucks, right? It sucks. So let's stop pointing out how much it sucks, and start coming up with solutions. If you don't have something positive to say, please keep it to yourself." Nat took a deep breath. "Anyone have any *constructive* ideas?"

The disappearance of their skis had complicated things in more ways than one. Not only had it effectively stranded them on the pass, but the one person who'd had the opportunity to take them was Igor, and the Russian couldn't have killed Joe and Anubha, since he'd been with her and Andrew at the other site when the trappers went missing. Igor swore that once Vasily returned from the forest, they hadn't been out of each other's sight. Not to mention that whoever had taken the skis had either taken them far or hidden them extremely well. The group had combed the Dyatlov Pass, the trail, and the forest as far as Lana's body, without finding so much as a single track.

The resulting silence was deafening, but she wasn't surprised. Take away the option of sniping at each other, and their "team" had nothing to say. If her job as a leader was to foster unity and inspire everyone to work collaboratively, she'd failed miserably.

"How about Joe and Anubha's snowshoes?" she asked.

Steven lifted his head, and she thought she detected at least a glimmer of interest. "What about them?"

"Well, they're better than nothing, right? Joe and Anubha moved pretty quickly in them."

"I hate to sound *negative*, but Joe and Anubha were just two people. There are five of us. So I'm not sure how their snowshoes, assuming we can find them, would help."

Argh, now his cloud of hopelessness had drifted over her way. "I thought we could trade off or something, have everyone take turns."

"I'm out," Igor said. "I cannot fit in their shoes."

"It's not practical, anyway. It would mean two of the group are either far ahead of the rest or waiting while the others struggle through the snow. Doesn't make sense, unless we plan on splitting up again, which I don't recommend."

Nat scowled at him, but Steven was right. It was probably worth saving the shoes, just in case, but trading them back and forth wouldn't make their progress any faster.

"I'm not meaning to come across as the Killer of All Hope here, but our resources are dwindling. In the time it will take us to walk down the mountain without our skis, assuming we don't get hit by a blizzard, we'll run out of food. We don't have enough."

"And whose fault is that?" Igor shot back, frowning at the mountaineer.

"It's no one's fault. It's simply a matter of supply and demand. We brought enough food to last a week, and we're getting to the end of the trip. It will take days, maybe even a week, to get anywhere on foot. Again, assuming good weather. No one planned for the skis to go missing."

"Maybe if you hadn't wasted all that food by leaving it out for the animals, we wouldn't be in this mess," Igor said. Nat was shocked at how angry the Russian looked, how flushed his face had gotten. She'd never seen him like this. Steven was on dangerous ground.

"I didn't leave it out for the animals. It was to appease the yetis, a peace offering to make up for hunting on their land. I did it to keep us safe."

"It didn't do much to keep Lana safe," Andrew muttered.

Steven turned on Andrew like a cornered cat. "I hope you're not blaming me for her death."

"I'm not blaming anyone. I'm agreeing with Igor that it was a stupid idea. Breakfast got ruined too." He held up a hand before Steven could jump down his throat. "I understand why, obviously. I'm just saying we shouldn't waste any more food."

"I don't think it was a waste. It might be the only reason the five of us are alive. Did anyone consider that? If we hadn't left the food, they might have ransacked our campsite and slaughtered all of us. Besides, if anyone had a problem with it, they should have said so last night, not today, when hindsight is 20/20."

"Would you have listened?" Igor asked. "From the first day, you have been telling us what to do and treating us like children. You've acted like this is your expedition, not Nat and Andrew's. Everyone else's suggestions are stupid. And yet, you're the one believing in children's fairy stories and leaving out food for yetis."

"How can you deny their existence? Who the hell else do you think took our skis?"

"*You* probably took them." Igor's voice rose until it was a roar. Nat had been about to ask the men to calm down, but now she was afraid to get between them. How had things gotten ugly so fast? "You're obsessed. Anubha and Joe died because they knew what you were up to. Lana died because she wasn't interested in you. You can off anyone who gets in your way, and blame it on the yeti." The Russian hooked his fingers into quotes as he said yeti. "Pretty fucking convenient."

"That's ridiculous. And, for your information, Lana was *plenty* interested." Steven smirked, and before Nat could blink, Igor lunged for him, grabbing him by the neck.

"You're a liar! That's a lie, and you know it. She was interested in *me*. She told me what you tried to do." Holding the mountaineer by the throat, Igor slammed Steven's head into the ground. "She told me you went into her tent that night. You're lucky I didn't kill you then."

Whaa? "Igor, *stop*. Please, someone stop him before he kills Steven."

Andrew and Vasily met her pleas with helpless expressions. It would have taken ten of them to have had a hope in hell. Shit. Steven had released Frankenstein's monster.

An eerie howl split the night air, starting off faint and growing louder and louder. It made the hairs on the back of Nat's neck stand on end. Igor froze with his hands wrapped around Steven's throat, Steven clawing at his fingers.

"What the fuck was that?" the Russian asked, but it came across as more of a demand than a question.

"I have told you what it is. Please stop—you are angering them with this fighting," Vasily said.

Igor groaned. "You expect us to believe that was a yeti?"

"Honestly, it sounded more like a wolf," Andrew said, and Nat agreed, although there'd been something unearthly, something inherently *wrong* about that sound. Then again, she'd heard the howls of wolves in the wild could be quite haunting. She'd never heard one before.

The guide wouldn't budge. "It is not a wolf. You are going to get us killed."

Whatever had made that noise had served its purpose. The rage that had infected Igor appeared to be gone. He let Steven go and stepped away from him, but before Nat could exhale, the Russian withdrew Joe's knife from his belt. "I assume I'm your next target, but I'm telling you now—anyone who comes into my tent tonight, man or beast, is going to get this in the heart. Understand?"

Steven scrambled to his feet, rubbing his neck and coughing. "I didn't kill anyone."

Something Igor had said troubled Nat. *She told me what you tried to do. She told me you went into her tent.* Had she unwittingly exposed Lana to a predator? And had the cheerful blonde died because of it? Her stomach twisted in knots.

"Steven, what happened with you and Lana? Did you—"

A horrified expression came over the mountaineer's face. "No! I don't know what she told Igor, but she *invited* me to her tent that night. We fooled around a bit, and then I left. I certainly didn't force myself on her. I would never do that."

"That's not what she told me." It made Nat nervous that Igor still held the knife, turning it over and over in his hands, as if he were considering his options.

"Maybe she didn't want to hurt your feelings."

"You know what? I think we should calm down, have some dinner, talk about less heated topics," Andrew said. "Otherwise, someone is going to end up dead, and it won't be because of any yeti."

"I'm sorry, but I can't drop this with you guys thinking I'm some sort of wannabe rapist. That's not fair. I really liked Lana, and would never have hurt her. Please believe me." Steven looked into her eyes, and even though Nat knew predators often dressed in sheep's clothing, she did believe him. Heaven help her.

"Unfortunately, Lana isn't here to give her side of the story, so we'll probably never know exactly what happened in her tent. But I believe Steven isn't a rapist," Nat said.

He nodded at her. "That's something, at least. Thank you."

"And I wish she, or someone, had told me what was going on. This was supposed to be my expedition, and I feel like there was a whole world going on behind the scenes that I didn't know about."

Andrew put his hand on her shoulder. "Isn't that always the way? The boss is the last to know."

"I suppose. But I'd hoped I wouldn't have to *be* a boss. I wanted us to get along, to be friends. To work as a team." Nat looked at what was left of her group, which Andrew had assembled with such pride. The Russian stood, knife in hand, like he expected to be attacked at any moment. Red welts had already appeared on Steven's throat. And Vasily, poor Vasily, looked as if he'd like nothing better than to melt into the ground and disappear.

"Well, that was never going to happen," Steven said, and everyone laughed. Even Vasily cracked a smile.

"Like it or not, we're stuck with each other. So we might as well make the best of it and try to survive. Igor, buddy, can you please put that knife away? You're making me nervous." Andrew slung his arm around Steven's shoulders, and Nat wasn't sure if it was out of affection or to protect him from the Russian. "What's for dinner?"

"I'm no Joe, obviously, but I'd suggest we crack open the cans of pork and beans. That way, we'll be without their weight tomorrow. Sound good?"

"You're asking for our opinion?" Nat feigned shock.

"Sure, there's a first time for everything," Steven said with a grin, thankfully taking her shot in the way it was meant.

Perhaps Igor's outburst, as terrifying as it was, had done some good.

"I think that sounds fantastic," Andrew said with more enthusiasm than canned beans deserved. "Igor, my friend, does that suit you?"

"Yah, I could eat." The Russian returned to his place by the fire, stabbing the knife into the ground by his feet. With the weapon taken out of play, Nat found she could breathe again, though her mind was spinning. How had she missed the drama between Lana, Igor, and Steven? She'd seen some flirting, but she'd thought that was the extent of it. Poor Lana. Had she pitted the two men against each other and died because of it? Or had she told Igor the truth? Even if Steven weren't a predator, he wouldn't have been the first man to have read a woman's signals wrong.

Nat's eyes filled at the thought of the vivacious Olympian. She missed the woman's sense of humor, her bright and easy chatter. From the start, Lana had provided much-needed comic relief. Nat doubted things would have gotten this dark if she'd been with them.

With supper sorted and Steven once again agreeing to cook for them, Andrew moved to sit beside her, bringing her close in a one-armed hug. She rested her head on his shoulder, using it as an excuse to hide her tears.

"I know," he said. "I miss her too."

~ CHAPTER FIFTEEN ~

The howling began in earnest that night. The ominous cries echoed over the campsite, chilling Nat in spite of her heavy parka, as the group's five remaining members clustered around the fire. She shivered in tandem with Andrew, who crouched beside her on the overturned log.

"Those aren't wolves," Igor said.

The color drained from Vasily's face. "No," he agreed. "Not wolves. It is the snowmen."

Nat braced herself for another outburst from the Russian about how the yetis were a fairy story, but the man kept his peace. Then again, it would have been difficult to argue with that horrible baying going on around them.

Removing her phone from her pocket, she hit the power button, only to be rewarded with a blank screen. "Fuck."

"Are you planning to record this?" Andrew asked. "Good idea."

"Well, I wanted to, but the battery's dead. I'll have to use the power packs to charge it." She left the rest of the sentence unsaid. No way she felt comfortable going back to the tent by herself.

"I think I should stay with you and Andrew tonight," Igor said, as if reading her mind. "It's not safe for us to be separated."

"What about me?" Steven asked.

"You can stay with Vasily. Perhaps your combined knowledge of yetis will protect you." The Russian stuck out his tongue.

"Very funny, but that's not fair. You have the only weapon," the mountaineer said. There was a frantic expression on his face that made Nat nervous.

"Vasily has his rifle. Besides, what happened to Lana wasn't fair." Igor shrugged.

"I told you, I had nothing to do with that. I loved her, okay? You happy now? I fucking *loved* her. I was going to ask her to move to California with me."

Nat's mouth dropped open, but before she could speak, there was another chorus of howls. Now she could hear snarling as well. Whatever was making that dreadful sound was getting closer.

"Please, please be quiet." Vasily raised his hands in the air. "You are going to get us all killed with your fighting."

"Maybe we shouldn't even go to bed tonight. Seems like that would make it easier for them, offering ourselves like pigs in a blanket," Andrew said.

Seeing Steven and Igor were on the verge of tearing each other apart, it was up to Nat to respond. "We aren't much safer out here."

"Aren't we? We could build the fire higher, make some torches. The torches could be our weapons, or maybe Vasily would let us take turns with his gun. At least out here we'd see what was coming. I don't know about you guys, but there's no way I'd get a wink of sleep, lying in that tent, wondering about who or what was creeping up on me."

Andrew's idea had some merit. She hadn't relished going inside for the night either. The image of Dyatlov's tent with its ruined side kept coming back to her. If their group hadn't gone to sleep that night, would they still be alive? "Sounds good to me. What do you guys think?"

"If they want to hurt us, they will hurt us," Vasily said. "It matters not whether we are inside the tent or outside."

"We can at least present a united front. Maybe if they see we're ready to fight, they'll leave us alone." Andrew selected a long stick from the firewood pile and stuck the tip of it into the fire. Nat guessed he was seeing how it would fare as a torch. "Maybe they've sensed weakness, and that's why they've been attacking us. Divide and conquer, and all that."

"They would snap that silly thing in half." Vasily curled his lip at the sight of Andrew's stick. "You do not understand what we are dealing with. These creatures have brute strength, and they are not dumb animals. You can't scare them off by waving a torch around."

Andrew's face reddened. "It was just an idea."

"We're basically fucked then, is what you're telling us, yah? We have no chance."

At Igor's words, Nat's mouth went dry.

Snowmen or not, some animal was out there, and it didn't sound friendly. She squirmed on the makeshift bench as her panic intensified. She didn't want to die; she wasn't ready. She had so many plans, so much left to do. "Why don't we take our chances with the mountain? It may be dark and cold, but it's better than sitting here waiting to die, isn't it?"

Steven shook his head. "They could be waiting for us out there, Nat. Guaranteed they know these mountains a hell of a lot better than we do. And if they're nocturnal hunters, they might be able to see in the dark as well."

"Well, what then? Sitting here doing nothing is driving me crazy."

Another chorus of howls made her jump. "Jesus Christ, that's awful."

"Vasily? If you're right about what these things are, you know the most about them. What do you suggest we do?" Andrew asked. The Mansi thought for a moment before raising his sad, brown eyes to her producer.

"I don't think there's anything we can do. They've gotten a taste for our blood."

"But Anubha, Joe, and Lana were killed, not eaten." Nat refused the memory of poor Anubha's mutilated face and Lana's contorted body. "It doesn't seem like they're using us for food. They could be killing us out of anger for encroaching on their territory, like Vasily said."

"Or maybe they enjoy it now, like the lions of Tsavo," Steven added. "The lions started out killing people for food, but ended up doing it for sport. For fun."

Andrew sighed. "I'd always hoped that if another sentient primate was discovered, it would have more sense than us, not less. But that sounds like us."

"Not to quibble over semantics, but there's no proof that these creatures are primates. Yetis have been described as resembling apes, but that might be because it's our only frame of reference for creatures that walk upright. The truth is, we know nothing about these animals or where they come from." Steven darted a look over his shoulder as a particularly shrieking cry pierced the air. "How are we supposed to fight an animal we know nothing about?"

There had to be something they could do. They were five skilled, intelligent people. Igor possessed incredible strength and size. Vasily was shrewd, with experience living in these mountains and surviving alongside the creatures, whatever they were. She and Andrew were talented problem solvers who could think on their feet. And Steven...well, she supposed he could always argue the creatures to death. What on earth had Lana seen in him, assuming he was telling the truth about that? Talk about polar opposites.

Maybe the key to their survival was hidden in the Dyatlov story, the reason they were there in the first place. "Let's go over what we know about the Dyatlov Pass incident. Judging by the condition of the tent and the way some of the bodies were poorly dressed for the elements, we can assume they were surprised during the night. For some reason, they couldn't leave normally, or they didn't feel safe doing so, so they cut through the nylon and escaped, running for the forest where we found Anubha and Joe."

"And the first bodies the searchers found were bruised and showed signs of a struggle," Steven said.

"Yes, just like Anubha, Joe, and Lana. So what does that tell us?" Nat had the odd sensation she was teaching a kindergarten class.

"The tents aren't safe," Igor said. "We'd be resting ducks."

"Sitting ducks, but close enough. Also, face-to-face confrontations don't work. If they did, Krivonischenko and Doroshenko would have survived. As would Anubha and Joe." She wracked her brain. There had to be a solution, some way out of this. But what?

"Maybe they weren't strong enough. Maybe someone like me would have a better chance."

"I wouldn't want to risk it, Igor. What if there's two, or three, or ten of them?" Andrew patted the Russian's arm. "Every man has his limits."

"The ones who lived the longest were the ones found under the snow," Nat said.

She saw a spark of recognition in Steven's eyes. "The ones who hid."

"Exactly. Unlike the Dyatlov group, we don't need weeks. We need to survive this one night, and then we can start making our way out of here. Maybe we'll run into a blizzard; maybe we'll starve. Maybe we'll get lost and fall off the side of the mountain. But we have to try. I don't know about you guys, but I'm not ready to die."

"Vasily? What do you think?" Steven asked. "You know these creatures better than anyone."

"It could work, if we had a good place to hide. But fighting, there is no chance. They are too strong." The Mansi stood and stretched. "We need to hurry. We are running out of time. It might already be too late."

"But where do we go? Where do we hide?" The anxiety on Andrew's face mirrored her own. It was dark and freezing, and they were surrounded by forest, a forest the creatures would be much more comfortable in and familiar with. A forest that held the corpses of their friends. It was tempting, so tempting, to crawl inside her nice, warm tent, get into her sleeping bag, and close her eyes. Had the Dyatlov group thought the same? Had they heard the howling but thought they'd be safe in their temporary homes?

"I believe I know a place that would work, but everyone needs to gather whatever supplies they can: blankets, warm clothing, food. It may be a while before we can come back." Vasily checked over his shoulder, just as a loud snarl made all of them jump. It sounded close. Dangerously close. "Hurry, hurry. There is not much time."

Without waiting to see if anyone agreed, the Mansi sprinted for his tent.

"If no one has any better ideas, I'd suggest we do as he says." Steven studied their faces, as though hoping someone *did* have a better idea. No one jumped to the challenge.

"At the end of the day, he's our guide. It's his job to keep us safe. I think we should listen to him," Nat said, and she was relieved when even Igor nodded. "Grab whatever you think will be useful and we'll meet back in five."

Sadly, they didn't have five.
As it turned out, they didn't even have three.

~ CHAPTER SIXTEEN ~

Panic didn't make a two-person tent easier to negotiate. After colliding with Andrew three times, she seized him by the upper arms.

"You—over there," Nat said, gesturing toward the back of the tent. "You stay in your corner, and I'll stay in mine."

"But some of my stuff is over there."

She snorted. "Do you think it matters at this point whose stuff is whose? Grab anything that looks useful and we'll sort it out later."

He hesitated, which unfortunately meant he kept blocking her path. "What if you forget something important?"

"I won't; I swear. You'll have to trust me. Now get."

True to her word, she scooped up Andrew's vast array of supplements and ointments and crammed them into her bag, though she knew Steven would have her head if he found out. Fuck him. He was done being the boss of her. Never should have been in the first place.

Bandages, nasal spray, extra socks, granola bars. Everything went into the pack. Nat's hands shook as she squashed it as flat as she could. They'd need all the room they could get.

"Hey, Nat?"

"Yeah?"

"Have room for this?"

It was Andrew's special travel pillow. Real goose down, from elusive Swiss geese or something like that. She didn't pause. Why not? It would probably be miserable enough where they were going. "Sure, fire it over."

Squashing the pillow into the pack's front pocket was more challenging than she'd expected. Nat was so consumed with the chore that it took her a moment to realize she no longer sensed movement from Andrew's half of the tent. She looked up to see him scribbling on a piece of paper.

"Andy, what on earth are you doing?"

He grinned. "Leaving a note for our rescuers."

What rescuers? Unlike Igor Dyatlov, she hadn't promised anyone a telegram. Or an email, for that matter. Out of the entire group, the first person to be missed would likely be Vasily. He was the one with family at home.

Andrew handed her the note.

From now on we know that snowmen exist.

"Very funny. How can you treat this as a joke?" But she knew. There was a feeling of unreality to the whole thing that made it difficult to take seriously. She'd been fighting the giggles all day, even after seeing Lana's poor battered body. Hysteria, that's what it was. They were all on the verge of hysteria.

"I don't know, Nat. Okay, obviously there's some kind of animal out there. I can hear them. *That*, I believe. Wolves, sure. Maybe some as-yet-undiscovered arctic hyena. But yetis? Abominable snowmen? Are we really going there?"

"Yeah, I think we are. Look, I get how bizarre this sounds—"

That's when they heard the screams.

Nat tore out of the tent, tripping over the threshold. Andrew was right behind her.

She froze on the spot, unable to move or cry out.

"What the fuck is that?" he breathed in her ear.

Some monstrous, hulking thing was dragging Vasily from his tent by the legs. The creature was massive, seven or eight feet tall. It wore a hooded coat of some kind of hide and had fur gloves on its hands. Nat couldn't see its face.

The Mansi shrieked, pleading for his life in his own language. Some things needed no translation.

"Oh my God," she whispered. This was happening. It was really happening. It wasn't a dream. It wasn't a nightmare. It was *real*.

From now on we know that snowmen exist.

With a howl of his own, Igor burst from his tent, shouting in Russian. Arm upraised, he rushed the creature, and before Nat could register what he was doing, he plunged Joe's knife into the thing's back. The creature screeched at a decibel level that threatened to puncture their eardrums. Nat and Andrew threw their hands over their ears while they watched the scene in horror.

The creature whipped around as though the six-inch knife were nothing but a nuisance, a mosquito bite. Flinging out its arm with an outraged squawk, it sent the Russian soaring at an impossible speed and height.

"Igor!" Nat cried.

She heard his screams as he vanished into the night, and the sickening thud as he hit the ground. Then nothing.

"You fucking piece of shit!"

Andrew seized a stick from the fire and charged the creature, using the makeshift torch like a spear, jabbing at its face.

"Andy, no!" Nat wanted to tackle him, to yank him away from that *thing*, but she couldn't move. It was as if her boots were nailed to the ground.

"Andrew, get away from that thing before it kills you," Steven said. Where had he come from?

Maybe a part of Andrew found the mountaineer attractive and wanted to impress him, even now. He gritted his teeth and launched his torch into the creature's face. This time, the thing squealed in pain, raising its arms to protect itself.

For a few seconds, everything stopped. Nat held her breath. Had Andrew done it? Had he hurt the creature enough to incapacitate it?

And then everything went crazy.

With a yowl of rage, the creature yanked the knife from its back and threw it on the snow. Then it went after Andrew.

"Holy shit!" Andy flew past her, diving into the tent. She heard the zipper close, and if Steven hadn't yanked her out of the way, the creature would have crashed right into her. Because of its hood, the thing's face was cloaked in shadow. Nat saw a glint of gold in the darkness as it rushed past.

Yellow eyes.

Before she could react, the creature raised its arm and clawed the tent, slicing it open. She heard Andrew yell for help.

The next moments were like a dream.

"Nat, no!"

Steven's warning didn't register. At that second, he didn't exist. Nothing did, except Andrew. And Andrew was in trouble.

Retrieving the knife from the ground, she ran at the creature, driving the blade deep into the thing's leg. It turned from the tent, growling and snarling, but she didn't wait to see what would happen next. Forcing the weapon from its flesh, she thrust it into the darkness beyond the hood, into where she'd seen that glint of gold. Hot liquid spurted from the wound as the creature shrieked.

Steven's arms were around her, pulling her back out of harm's way. The creature toppled face first onto the snow, its horrible cries dying with it.

Nat shoved the mountaineer away, breaking free from his grip. "Andrew, Andrew, are you okay?" Her hands shook so badly she almost couldn't unzip the tent. But then she was inside and her friend was in her arms and he was crying and he was alive—oh my God, he was alive.

"Nat." Andrew took her face in his hands, the nylon from his gloves scratching her cheek. "You saved my life, you crazy bitch."

"Don't you ever, *ever* do that again, you hear me?"

He laughed through his tears. "I don't think you have to worry about that. My heroic days are over."

"Thank fuck for that."

"Hey." Steven burst into their tent, pale and distraught. It spooked them so much they started laughing again. "He's okay?"

Andrew winked. "I'm fine. Probably took a few years off my life, but I do that pretty well on my own anyway."

"Well, good. I'm glad. Because Igor is not okay. I need your help. Both of you."

Fuck. Igor. In all the turmoil, she'd temporarily forgotten about him. "Let's go."

Steven led the way past the fire. Igor lay near the trail, covered with a blanket. He raised his head when he heard them coming, and Nat wanted to weep with relief. She hadn't expected him to have survived.

"I'm sorry, Nat."

She fell to her knees in the snow beside him. "What are you sorry for? You're a hero. You saved Vasily's life. Wait a minute—where is Vasily? Has anyone seen him?"

Steven shook his head. "I've been preoccupied with Igor. I assume he's in his tent, probably afraid to come out."

Igor's breathing was ragged, and his forehead shone with sweat, but otherwise he looked all right. "Are you in pain, Igor? Can you move?"

"I think I broke my leg, Nat. Hurts like hell."

Shit. There went their plan of walking down the mountain tomorrow. And of Igor helping Andrew. Now she understood why he'd apologized, though it wasn't his fault. "Can you wiggle your toes?"

He moved one foot but yelped when he attempted the other.

"Okay, let's move him by the fire. At least I'll have a bit more light," she said.

"Do you have a first aid kit?" Steven asked, the hope in his voice palpable.

"Only the basics. I have gauze and we can make splints from some sticks. It should be enough to make do until we can get him some real medical help." Steven's eyes met hers and she could guess what he was thinking: what medical help? And what if it weren't only Igor's leg that was hurt? What if he had internal bleeding or worse? Thankfully, the mountaineer kept his mouth shut for a change. "Let's see if we can move him, and then we'll go check on Vasily. Steven, do you have another blanket? I'm thinking we can gently slide him along the snow."

"I'll go get one." He sprinted for his tent, snow flying from his boots.

"I thought you weren't supposed to move people," Andrew whispered. "What if his back is broken?"

"Well, I don't see any paramedics here, do you? We have no choice." She bent over Igor again, brushing his sweat-soaked hair off his forehead. "How are you feeling? Up to moving by the fire?"

"The fire would be nice. I-I'm freezing."

His teeth chattered, although his skin was hot to the touch. Great. Did that mean he was in shock? What were you supposed to do for people in shock? She wished she'd taken more courses, or at least paid better attention to the ones she had.

"Hang on. Steven's gone to get a blanket we can use as a kind of sled. We'll try our best not to hurt you, but it's probably going to hurt a bit, okay?"

"Okay." He gripped her hand with surprising strength. No spinal injury, then. He could wiggle his toes and control his upper body. It was a relief, though a broken leg would make traversing the mountain all but impossible. Still, it could have been so much worse.

Steven returned with a wool blanket. Taking off his belt, he held it up to the Russian's mouth. Igor stared at him in confusion. "Bite this so you don't scream. We don't know how many more creatures are out there, and we certainly don't want to call any of them."

As Igor took the belt between his teeth, Nat had the overwhelming sensation she was in a movie. How many times had she seen some Western or action flick where a man bit down on a belt to keep from crying out? She'd never expected to experience it in real life.

When the second blanket was spread flat on the snow, the three paused for a moment, examining their patient. How would they move him without killing him? Igor had to weigh at least two hundred and twenty pounds, maybe more. He was a huge man, a mountain of muscle. Andrew hadn't yet regained his strength, so it would be up to her and Steven. She saw her own doubts reflected in the mountaineer's eyes.

"Can you roll onto the blanket, buddy?" Steven knelt at Igor's feet, holding the blanket straight.

"I can try."

Grunting, Igor half rolled, half scooted onto the blanket. His jaw clenched as he clamped down on the belt, and the sweat poured off him. Once he'd made it, he flopped straight back, panting.

"You're amazing, man. You're a machine." Andrew clapped.

Nat had broken her wrist before, and she well remembered the sickening pain, the waves of nausea. She couldn't imagine how much worse a broken leg would be.

"Are you all right, Igor?"

He spit the leather from his teeth. "Yah, I'll be fine. Just give me a minute."

"Once we get some momentum going, pulling him should be fairly easy," Steven said. "But I'm worried about Vasily."

"Do you want to check on him now? Andrew can go with you while I stay with Igor."

"No, let's not split up again. We'll deal with this first, and then look for Vasily."

Nat shuddered, picturing the creature dragging the Mansi from his tent. Vasily had been terrified, but he hadn't appeared to be hurt. She hoped she was right about that.

"Okay, let's get this party started." Igor propped himself up on his elbows while Andrew rearranged a blanket over his body. Steven and Nat each picked up a corner of the cloth near the Russian's feet, while Andrew stood behind his back, ready to help when and however necessary. At Steven's nod, he held the belt so Igor could take it between his teeth again.

"Let's do this slow and gentle. If we go too fast, we could end up pulling this thing right out from under him."

For once she didn't feel an urge to hit Steven for stating the obvious. His voice was soothing and she needed to be soothed. "Right."

"On the count of three. One...two...three."

At first, nothing happened. Nat leaned into it until her back strained and her vertebrae popped, and then slowly, slowly, the blanket began to move. Her feet slipped in the snow as she struggled to get traction.

"You all right?" Steven asked, but she had no excess energy left to speak. She managed a grunt while Igor moaned.

"You're doing great, buddy. Doing great. Almost there." Andrew was at his most encouraging. "Guys, he's not looking so good. Can we move a little faster?"

Steven had been right. Now that they'd gotten started, it was much easier to pull, but they needn't have worried about yanking the blanket out from under the Russian. The man was too heavy. They steadily picked up speed, closing the distance between the trailhead and the fire. Within a minute or two, Nat could feel the welcoming heat on her skin. She helped the mountaineer pull Igor alongside.

The Russian had looked better in the dark. In the flickering light of the fire, his skin was gray. She hoped it was an illusion. Sweat poured down his face as he gasped for air. Lowering herself to the snow, she stroked his head. "Andrew, can you get me a towel, please?"

He nodded and ran off while the Russian continued to moan. "Don't worry, Igor. We're going to splint your leg. Hopefully that will help with the pain."

"No..." he managed, wincing. "No, please. Not yet."

"Okay, we'll wait for a bit. Try to relax. Are you comfortable? Well, as much as you can be?" Andrew was back with the towel, and Nat used it to wipe off Igor's face. She was struck by how young he was. In pain and helpless, he looked closer to his actual age of twenty-four than usual. She'd forgotten he wasn't much more than a kid. Although she wasn't a religious person, she said a quick prayer in her mind that she would be able to return Igor to his family, whole and healthy.

"Nat?"

"Mmm-hmm?" Steven had been so quiet she'd forgotten he was there.

"We have a problem."

"What is it?" she asked, though she'd have given anything not to know. Ignorance was most definitely bliss, but it was also a luxury she couldn't afford.

"I went ahead and checked on Vasily. He's gone. Along with his gun. The creature you killed is gone too."

And then there were four.

~ CHAPTER SEVENTEEN ~

Steven sat beside Igor with the blood-encrusted knife in his hand. His attention moved to her when she stirred.

"Good morning," he whispered.

"Good morning."

At the sight of him sitting there, keeping watch while the rest of them slept, guilt overwhelmed her. Taking a deep breath to steady her voice, she surveyed the campsite and noticed the towering pile of wood heaped just beyond the fire.

"Wow, you've been busy."

"I can't take the credit for that. I was too scared to leave you, so Andrew did it."

Andrew. She glanced at her sleeping producer, her best friend. He was zonked out, mouth open, snoring away. Whoever would have thought that could sound beautiful?

"That took some balls, going back in the forest last night." As nice as the stockpile was, she wished he hadn't taken the risk.

"He stuck to the outskirts. Took a lot of courage, though. Not sure I could have done it."

Pushing her sleeping bag from her legs as quietly as she could, she tensed when the cold air hit her sleep-warmed body. She stepped around Andrew to sit beside the mountaineer, holding her hands to the fire.

"That's nice of you to say, but we both know you're the bravest person here."

He gave her a bemused smile. "I thought I was the Antichrist."

"I'm so sorry, Steven. For doubting you, and for accusing you. I'm—I'm ashamed at how we treated you."

"It's okay. I think a situation like this would make anyone paranoid. And it's not like I gave you any reason to trust me." He stared at the fire, not meeting her eyes.

"Even so. A troll and a murderer are two different things."

"Don't forget rapist."

Her hand flew up to cover her face. "Oh my God, I'm sorry. I was a total shit to you."

He bumped his shoulder against hers. "It's okay, really. I'm glad you see the truth now, because we're not going to survive this unless we work together."

Nat looked over at Igor, but the man was so covered with blankets and sleeping bags she couldn't see his face. "How's he doing?"

"Okay, I think. His coloring is a lot better this morning, and his breathing sounds good. Hopefully it's a clean break and we can get it set today. It's not ideal, but it won't be fatal."

Now that she could view it in the light of dawn, their campsite resembled the aftermath of a horror movie. There were pools of dark crimson around her tent and Vasily's, and more blood leading away from the scene. The tattered side of her tent flapped in the wind.

"Seems familiar, doesn't it?" He gestured at her tent, which had been sliced cleanly open.

"Dyatlov's."

"You know, it's always bothered me, that cut in the side of the tent. It drove me crazy, wondering why they didn't leave through the entrance."

"And now we know."

"All that talk about avalanche paranoia and infrasound making them insane, and it was yetis the whole time," Steven said.

"Do you think that's what that thing was? A yeti?"

"What else would you call it?"

She wrapped her arms around herself, feeling cold in spite of the fire's warmth when she thought of those gold eyes. She'd only caught a glimpse of them, but a glimpse had been more than enough. "I'm not sure. I guess I didn't expect them to be so humanoid. I'd always thought yetis would be covered with fur."

"Did you get a look at the one you killed?"

"Did I kill it, though? I thought I did—put that knife right through its eye." She shuddered at the memory. "But if it's dead, where did it go?"

"I think the others took it, along with Vasily. They can't leave any bodies behind. If there are bodies, there's proof." Steven stirred the embers, quietly adding more wood.

"Shit. I was hoping there was only the one."

"Wishful thinking, but you heard the howls last night. I'm thinking there's a pack of them."

"Fuck. What are we going to do?" That desperate, I-don't-want-to-die panic caught her by the throat again, making it difficult to speak.

"To be honest, I'm not sure. We can't leave today, obviously." Steven's gaze settled on the blanket-wrapped mound that was Igor. "So I guess we'll have to hide."

"Hide where?"

"What about the ravine?" Andrew sat up, startling them both.

Nat pressed her hand against her chest, silently willing her heart to keep beating. "You scared the shit out of me."

"Sorry, we tried not to wake you," Steven said.

"It's okay. The sun did a fine job of that on its own." Andrew yawned and stretched. "What time is it?"

Steven checked his watch before squinting at the sun, pretending to study it. "I don't know…around eight?"

"Very funny. I can't believe I slept that long. I didn't think I'd be able to close my eyes after everything that happened."

"Well, you got a lot of exercise yesterday." Nat tilted her head at the woodpile. "Nice work, by the way."

"Thanks. Yeah, it figures. I'm finally in the shape I've always wanted to be, and there's no one around to appreciate it."

Steven stood up from the log. "Now that the two of you are up, guess I might as well start breakfast."

She put her hand on his arm. "Let me do it this time. There's no reason you have to cook for us every day."

"I don't mind, but since you insist…"

"I insist. Where's the stuff?"

"It's in Joe's backpack, in my tent." Seeing her hesitation, he asked, "Want me to get it?"

Mentally shaking herself, she stood, eyeing Steven's tent like it was a guillotine. "No, it should be fine. It's daylight and we're all here; what could go wrong?"

Andrew tsk-tsked under his breath. "Don't tempt fate, Nat."

It was silly. Clearly, there was nothing ominous about the tent. She'd be able to see a creature lurking outside, or even inside, and Steven was right there with the knife. Andrew would never let anything happen to her. So what was she afraid of?

Squaring her shoulders, Nat forced herself to adopt her most confident walk, putting a little swing in her hips. She knew both men were watching her. For some reason it was important to show them that she could do this simple thing without their help.

The sour-sweet smell of blood made her wrinkle her nose as she got closer. She averted her eyes, hoping it wasn't Vasily's. Steven's tent gave off a seriously bad vibe; there was no doubt about it. She could tell herself she was being ridiculous, or that it was her imagination getting carried away, but her instincts hadn't steered her wrong so far. It would be foolhardy to mistrust them now.

"You sure you don't want me to get it?" Steven called.

"I'm fine." She unzipped the flap.

His tent was dim and musky with the smell of man. Nat blinked, waiting a second or two for her eyes to adjust. Grabbing the first backpack she saw, she knelt and unzipped it, but as she started going through it, she quickly saw it was the wrong one.

The main compartment was full of underwear: lacy, silky, girly things. Not what you'd expect a man to bring on a camping trip. Still, everyone had their kink. Who was she to judge Steven's? As she stuffed the panties back inside, her face burning, she spotted one pair that didn't belong. Gray, sporty boy shorts. Hers. She hadn't noticed they were missing.

"Are you having trouble finding it?"

Nat jumped, biting her lip so she wouldn't cry out. She barely had time to cram her underwear back in the bag before Steven lifted the tent flap and stepped inside. "Yeah, I think I've got the wrong pack."

Their eyes met, and she saw he knew what she'd seen. What would he do? Would he lie, or come up with some lame excuse for stealing her underwear? She was relieved the knife wasn't in his hand. Hopefully he'd left it with Andrew.

"Find anything interesting?"

"Nothing I haven't seen before."

He took the bag from her hands. "That's Lana's pack. Joe's is over here."

"Oh." While he was turned away getting Joe's bag, she took a steadying breath. Why would Lana have her underwear? And how stupid did Steven think she was? Lana's pack had been fire-engine red. Steven's was black.

"Breakfast burrito or beef tips?"

"Huh?"

Steven smiled at her, his teeth reminding her of a shark's. "We're not exactly spoiled for choice anymore. After yesterday's attempt, I'm not sure I could stomach another breakfast burrito. Think anyone will complain about the beef tips? They're not technically breakfast food."

Beef tips. *Fuck.* Was everything that came out of his mouth going to sound like a euphemism now? She cleared her throat. "I'm sure they'll be fine. I think we're all just feeling lucky to be alive at this point."

"True. All right, executive decision. Beef tips it is." He pulled the silver packets from Joe's pack. "Hope you're not offended I came to check on you. I realized how many bags I have in here. It can get confusing if you don't know what's what."

He could say that again. It was damn confusing. "No problem. I understand."

She was eager to leave the tent, uneasy about Steven's following behind. The cold air was beautiful and fresh after spending a few minutes in that dank, foul-smelling cave. Ugh. What if Lana had told

Igor the truth about Steven's coming into her tent uninvited? Now that she thought about it, her face flushed with shame. How could she have ever doubted Lana? Lana wouldn't have lied about something like that. And here Nat had suspected her of playing two men at the same time. She felt terrible.

"You survived," Andrew said, and she made herself relax, not wanting to let him know anything was wrong. Not yet, not with Steven right behind her. "And look who else is awake."

"Good morning." The Russian had deep purple shadows under his eyes, and his blond stubble made him appear paler than normal, but Nat thought he was about the most gorgeous thing she'd ever seen. It was almost enough to make her forget about the backpack.

Almost.

"Good morning, Igor. Am I ever happy to see you." Giving Steven a wide berth, she went to the Russian and hugged him gently around the chest and shoulders, careful not to jostle his leg. "How are you feeling?"

"Sore, but okay. Hungry."

"I'll take care of that right away." She wished he could read her mind. *Lana told you the truth. Steven is a predator.* The Russian's brow furrowed. He could tell she was troubled, but she was sure he didn't know why. And unless Steven decided he needed to go back to his tent, there would be no opportunity to tell the others what she'd found.

"That's all right. Why don't you keep Igor entertained while I make breakfast? I really don't mind. I'm kind of getting into this nurturing shit," Steven said, ripping open a foil packet and pouring it into the cook pot, which was already full of boiling water.

"Are you sure?" She hoped her tone managed to convey, *Don't think this lets you off the hook.*

"Yes, I'm sure. Let me be useful. That way I won't get voted off the island."

"I don't think it's us you have to impress," Andrew said. "We're not the ones doing the voting."

"Are you okay?" Igor mouthed, and she squeezed his hand, while shaking her head the tiniest bit.

Not now. She cut her eyes to Steven, and trusted the Russian understood. More than anything, she wished he wasn't injured. He was their protector, their muscle. If Steven decided to turn on them, to "vote them off," who would stop him?

"So, Nat. You never did answer my question."

It was all she could do to keep from cringing. Steven's voice, which had been so welcome not that long ago, now set her teeth on edge. She met Andrew's eyes, and he winked at her, back to his happy, playful self. *He has my panties*, she wanted to scream. *He attacked Lana.*

"Which question is that?" Andrew asked.

"Before you two sleeping beauties were awake, she mentioned that she hadn't expected our new friends to be human in appearance, so I asked her if she got a good look at the one she killed, but she hasn't answered me yet. Trying to keep me in suspense, I suppose."

"No, I just forgot." Her head spinning, it was impossible to focus, but finally the nightmare she'd seen the night before came back to her. The hooded patchwork-type coat, the glowing eyes, the metallic-sounding shrieks, like metal grating on metal. "Not really. I only saw its eyes."

"What did they look like?" Igor asked. "I just saw its back, and then its arm as it sent me into space." He shifted on the blankets, wincing. "I'm hoping I'll be the last thing *it* sees, the fucker."

"Nat killed it. Didn't you know?" Andrew sounded thrilled to be the bearer of the good news. "It's dead."

"If it's dead, why are we asking her what it looked like? Where is it?"

"Sadly, we don't know." Steven tapped his spoon against the side of the pot. "It disappeared while we were helping you. Along with Vasily." His blue eyes pinned Nat to the spot. *I had nothing to do with that.*

But she wasn't so sure. How could she be sure of anything now?

The Russian whistled under his breath. "Fuck."

"Its eyes were yellow. Or maybe gold. No pupils that I could see."

"That's creepy," Andrew said.

"Could you see its nose?" Igor asked, grinding his fist into his palm as though he'd love another shot at the creature.

"No. It was too dark, and it had that big hood. All I saw were the eyes. And believe me, that was enough."

"Yellow eyes with no pupils. That doesn't sound very human, does it?" Steven said. He smiled at her again, but there was no humor in it. In fact, it gave her the willies. In that moment, she would have gladly taken her chances with the creature.

"No. Not human at all."

~ CHAPTER EIGHTEEN ~

The food formed a lump in her stomach. Finding her underwear in Steven's pack had killed her appetite, but they had so few meals left. She couldn't waste it, even though every bite tasted like cardboard and she could feel his eyes burning into her.

She was so confused. At first, she'd thought Steven was the bad guy, then he'd been a good guy, and now he was the bad guy again. Maybe no one was good *or* bad, but a myriad of puzzling shades of gray.

"You have to leave me."

Nat started when Igor spoke. The tension between her and Steven must have infected everyone else, because for the last while, everyone had stared into the fire in gloomy silence. Even Andrew appeared to be at a loss for words.

"What are you talking about?" he said now. "We're not leaving you."

"You have to. It's the smart thing to do." He gestured at his blanket-covered leg, and Nat realized they still had no idea how bad the injury was. She hoped the bone hadn't broken through the skin, increasing the Russian's chances of infection. "I can't walk, and you guys have to leave. You have to get out of here today. They'll return tonight, wanting revenge for their friend. If you stay, you'll die."

Andrew got that stubborn expression on his face she was all too familiar with. "We're not leaving you to die."

"He's right, so you might as well stop talking nonsense, Igor," she said, lending her will to Andrew's before Steven could speak up and say that actually, abandoning one of the last remaining members of their group was a capital idea. "If you're not going, we're not going."

"You can hide me. Hide me in that ravine Andrew's talking about. Splint my leg, and maybe I'll manage to survive until it heals enough for me to leave. That gives me as good a chance as I'd have trying to get down the mountain with you."

Right, the ravine. "What ravine?"

"The ravine—you know, the one Lyudmila and her friends hid in." Andrew's eyes shone the way they always did when he thought he'd come up with a brilliant idea.

"Have you forgotten what happened to Lyudmila?" The memory was enough to make her stomach churn. All that blood she'd swallowed, proving the poor girl had still been alive when her tongue and the inside of her mouth were removed.

"They survived the longest. It might buy us a night or two, maybe more. Plus, we don't know what happened. Maybe they made too much noise or something, and that's how the creatures found them. We wouldn't make any noise."

The prospect of hiding in Lyudmila's grave was far from comforting. "Andy, we have no idea where the ravine is. And, even if we manage to find it—and that's a big if—what if the creatures remember where they found Lyudmila and her friends? What if that's the first place they think to look?"

"I'm assuming they have life cycles. They bleed, they hurt, they die—they're not immortal. They're not magic. It's unlikely that the ones who are terrorizing us are the same ones who murdered the Dyatlov group."

"Maybe not, but the bodies of Joe, Anubha, and Lana were clearly posed to recreate what happened in the past. So if it's not the same creatures, that knowledge has been passed on."

"Reports describe the ravine as being two hundred and fifty feet deeper into the woods past the cedar tree where we found Joe and Anubha," Steven said. "We should be able to find it."

"Or break our own legs in the process," Nat said. "I don't think we should hide. I think we should fight."

Igor wrinkled his brow. "Fight? Fight how? You've seen how strong these things are. That one threw me over fifteen feet like I weighed nothing. What chance do we have against that kind of power?"

"They may be stronger, but I'm willing to bet we're smarter." Nat steeled herself for a battle. She'd suspected it wouldn't be easy to convince them, but her instincts told her it was the right thing to do. When they'd minded their own business, the creatures had picked them off one by one. But when they'd fought back, they were left alone. All it took was the death of one snowman to force the creatures into a retreat.

Steven chuckled. "I wouldn't take that bet. Humans are the dumbest species in existence."

She decided to ignore him. Enough with his naysaying. He'd argue what color the sky was if it suited him. "There have to be things we can do, traps we can set, weapons we can make. Think about it—they could have returned and killed us last night, but they didn't. They took their dead and left. They attack the weak, don't you see that? If we're not weak, they might leave us alone. And I don't know about you, but I'm tired of being weak. I want to kick some yeti *ass*."

"They also took Vasily," Andrew said.

"More reason for us to fight back. They've killed four of our friends. Do we really want to roll over and let them kill the rest of us?"

"I get what you're saying, Nat. And if my leg weren't buggered, I might agree with you. But I've felt the power of these creatures—you haven't. And I honestly think the only shot we have is for you three to hide me and get the fuck out of here before they come back."

For some reason, Igor's resignation angered her more than Steven's devil's advocate routine. Was she the only one who wasn't a coward? What was wrong with them? "You're right. I haven't felt their power, but I *have* felt their weakness. I stabbed one through the eye and killed it. If I can kill one, I can kill more."

"Not trying to take anything away from you, but you did have the advantage of surprise," Steven said. "You won't have that next time. They'll be ready for you. And we only have one knife."

She rolled her eyes. "Obviously I'm not going to try the exact same strategy again. And there are other things we could use as weapons. We have climbing gear, cooking utensils, and tools. There has to be something. But I seem to be the sole person interested in standing up to these fuckers."

Steven sighed, rubbing his forehead. "My interest has always been in doing what's best for the group as a whole, trying to ensure that the greatest number of us survive."

"And how's that working for you?" she shot back.

"Nat, that isn't fair. It's not Steven's fault four people are dead." Andrew shook his head at the number. It seemed impossible that half of their group was gone, but that very fact galvanized her. Didn't they get that?

"I never meant to imply that. I'm simply suggesting that what we've been doing so far clearly isn't working. And since I'm the one who saved your life last night, I'd hoped you'd listen to me."

"I *am* listening to you. I'm sorry, but it sounds kind of mad. What do you want us to do, charge these things armed with cooking pots and ski poles, assuming we still have some poles lying around somewhere? Maybe if there were twenty or thirty of us it would work, but with four? Our one hope would be to render them helpless with laughter."

"Don't be ridiculous," she said, doing her best to ignore Steven's smirk. "I wouldn't suggest anything that insane. But I do think that with some planning we can beat these things, or at least scare them off so they leave us alone."

"Do you have a plan, Nat? Are you thinking of anything in particular?" The fact Andrew was taking her seriously, or was willing to hear her out, was enough. He wouldn't let her down. They'd worked together and been friends for too long. He knew, better than anyone, that she didn't have stupid ideas.

"I do," she said. "But the first step is to fix Igor's leg. And then I'm going to see if I can charge our phones and get a signal."

* * *

"Maybe he'll cause an avalanche with all that screaming, and then we don't have to worry about the yetis," Andrew joked, but paled when the Russian lunged at him. Her producer doubled back so fast he tripped and almost fell on his ass.

Igor's face darkened with rage as he spat foreign words at them around the belt Steven kept wedged between his teeth. "No such luck," the mountaineer said. "I think we're done."

To Nat's relief, the bone hadn't broken through the skin, but Steven had diagnosed it as a "bad break" of the tibia. She'd always thought that was an odd expression. What on earth was a "good break"?

Splinting the leg began with her and Andrew trying to hold Igor down while the mountaineer gently tugged on the limb until it was straight. Her ears still rang from the Russian's ear-blistering shrieks of pain.

Igor leaned to one side and threw up on the snow. So much for the beef tips.

"Almost done, big guy. Just a bit more gauze."

She'd found Joe's carved walking stick in the couple's tent. The workmanship was stunning, and it hurt to chop it in two to make the splint. But she had a feeling the trappers would have understood.

No one had ever had a more elegant splint. If nothing else, they'd done Igor proud.

"Tape, please?" Steven asked, and Nat gave it to him, careful not to make contact with his skin. Once again, she struggled to reconcile her feelings about him. One minute, he was a sexual deviant; the next, the closest thing they had to a medic. He'd set Igor's leg like a pro. If they could get the creatures to back off, the Russian's tibia could possibly heal enough for them to get safely home. "There you go. How you feelin', man?"

Igor glowered at him. "How the fuck do you think I'm feeling? You bloody torturer."

"Hey, I get that it's not fun, but we had no choice. You'll thank me later, when you're back teaching chicks how to ski with your nice, straight legs."

"Maybe. But in the meantime, I'd get out of my sight for your own safety."

Steven threw up his hands. "I can't win with you people." Glancing at the fire, his face fell. "And we're almost out of wood again. Nat, will you help me, please?"

Startled, Nat looked to Andrew, hoping he could read her mind.

"It's okay," he said, failing her utterly. "You two go ahead. I'll stay with Igor and keep him company."

Clearly, they'd have to work on their telepathy if they ever got out of this mess.

She fell behind Steven on the trail, keeping her distance as they trudged to the edge of the woods. Her heart was beating uncomfortably fast. What if he tried to hurt her? Did he have the knife? Tucking her hands in her pockets, she felt around for anything she could use as a weapon if it came to it. Some tissue, a tube of lip balm, and a pen. Clenching the pen in her fist, she vowed to jab it into his eye if he so much as looked at her funny.

She was so focused on her plan that she almost ran right into his back. "What's wrong? Why did you stop?"

"Listen, Nat. I didn't really need your help to gather the wood. I wanted to talk to you."

Tightening her grip on the pen, she nodded. "I kind of figured that."

"Things have been tense between us since you went in my tent, and I've got a pretty good idea why. For the record, I'm really embarrassed you saw that. I'm sure I must seem strange to you."

Was he serious? "No, strange isn't the word I'd use."

He reached for her arm, and when she jerked it away, his face crumpled. "It isn't what you think. That...clothing you found, it's Lana's. It may sound silly, but she was such a private person. After my aunt and her friends disappeared, a team of searchers came up here and went through all their things. Some stuff—personal items—went missing, including a journal. I couldn't stand the thought of anyone pawing through Lana's private things, making crude comments about them. I was determined to survive and make sure no one saw them but me."

It was a pretty speech, and if someone else had made it, Nat might have believed it. "That would make a lot of sense, except for the fact that you also have my underwear. Please don't tell me you're stockpiling *my* panties for safekeeping, because if rescuers arrive to save my life, I couldn't give a rat's ass what they say about my undies."

She got a little satisfaction watching the color drain from his face.

"There must be some mistake."

"I'd say the whole thing is a mistake, but it wasn't me who made it. I hope you're not about to suggest I don't know my own underwear. It's easy to spot, since it's a departure from the rest of your collection. I assumed you'd wanted some variety from the lacy, frilly stuff."

"C'mon, Nat. Do I strike you as some kind of creepy panty sniffer? I swear, anything I took was from Lana's tent, and I did it to protect her. If somehow a pair of yours got into the mix, then they were with her things." He clapped a hand to his forehead. "Argh, this is more embarrassing than I thought. I can only imagine what you must be thinking of me."

"Trust me, you don't want to know." She'd started off with a strong conviction never to believe him again, but now his story was wearing on her. Could he be telling the truth?

"I would never violate your privacy that way. Lana and I were lovers; it was different. I promise you that she'd be okay with what I did. Otherwise, I never would have done it."

"Lovers? Is that what you call rape these days?" The words were out of her mouth before she could stop them. She watched Steven warily. He could crush her windpipe before she had the chance to scream. But instead of looking angry, the mountaineer appeared horrified.

"Rape? Are we back to that again? I never raped anyone. Why would you say that? Even if you think I stole your underwear, that doesn't make me a rapist."

"Why else would Lana have told Igor you forced yourself into her tent? While she didn't say rape, it was strongly implied."

Steven removed his cap to run his hand through his dark hair. It was sickening that even now, he managed to look handsome. "I wish she were here to explain some of these things herself. Lana was a sweet girl, but sometimes her naïveté got her into trouble. She told me Igor had made some advances, was coming on strong. Since we were stuck with each other for the week, she didn't want to hurt his feelings. She was desperate to avoid any bad blood. So she told him she was gay. That worked pretty well until Igor saw me going into her tent one night."

As much as she didn't want to believe him, Nat could picture it. The crestfallen expression of betrayal on Igor's face, Lana's verbal tap dancing to explain her relationship with Steven while keeping the peace. But still, Lana claiming Steven had forced his way into her tent could have gotten the mountaineer killed. "Why would she say it wasn't consensual, though? You're lucky Igor didn't wring your neck."

"Well, according to what she told me, that isn't *quite* what she said. She said we were friends, and that I wanted more from the relationship than she did. Which was probably true. I was more than willing to relocate to Canada if she didn't fancy moving to California. Lana was quite hesitant, said we were rushing things."

Nat raised an eyebrow. "I'd say. You'd only known her a few days."

He shrugged, kicking at a crust of snow. "Doesn't matter. When you know, you know. There isn't another woman like her in the world. I'd stake my life on it."

It was his tone, the sincerity in his eyes, that convinced her. As creepy as his panty hoarding was, there was no doubt in her mind that he'd loved Lana, and loved her very deeply. Whether or not Lana had felt the same was anyone's guess. "Once again, it seems I owe you an apology for leaping to conclusions. But it was so startling to find my underwear in that pack. Especially since I was looking for the breakfast burritos."

A smile played at the corner of his lips. "No problem. This has been so mortifying that I'd be perfectly happy to forgive and forget. Deal?"

"Deal."

"So, with that out of the way and my fledgling reputation as the Great Panty Bandit of Dead Mountain laid to rest, will you tell me your plans for tonight?"

"Later. First, we need to gather firewood. *A lot* of firewood. Once we rejoin the others, I'll explain everything."

"Okay, I guess I can remain in suspense for that long." Steven knelt to gather branches that had fallen during a previous storm, but not before Nat caught him wiping his eyes.

"Steven?"

"Yeah?" His voice was a bit rougher than usual, and in spite of her misgivings, her heart went out to him.

"I'm sorry about Lana. She was a wonderful woman."

"Thanks. She felt the same way about you."

~ CHAPTER NINETEEN ~

"Are you sure about this?" Steven's eyes locked with hers as he held the knife over her skin.

She nodded. "Yes."

"It could get infected."

"Are you kidding? That swill Igor drinks would kill anything." She'd expected more grumbling about Igor's great sacrifice, but the Russian had told her where to find his stash without a fight. "Hey, if this works, I'll never drink again," he'd said, and from the conviction in his voice, he might have even believed it. She was just thankful there were no ladies' unmentionables in *his* bag.

"True. Okay, you asked for it."

With a deep breath, Steven sliced the blade across her thumb, where a cut would bleed without nicking an artery. The knife was so sharp Nat felt nothing at first, followed immediately by fire. She turned her hand over, squeezing her flesh, and watched her blood spatter on the floor of the tent.

"I don't understand why you're doing this. We've already agreed to sacrifice our last packet of beef tips."

She grinned. "Just upping the ante. How are the stakes coming along?" In truth, it was partly penance. She'd been horrified to discover that every single power pack she'd brought to charge the phones was useless, drained. There wasn't much of a chance of getting a signal in the mountains, but even so, the power packs had represented one of their last hopes, and now they were gone too. Why hadn't she checked them earlier?

"Great, actually. Who knew Igor was such a whittler?"

"It's amazing what talents one uncovers when people are motivated."

"True. I only hope it's enough."

"Steven..." He'd promised her to can the negative talk. Her plan was a bit crazy, a bit arts 'n' crafts, and it was cobbled together from a few different horror movies, but it was a hell of a lot better than sitting around a campfire waiting to die. And she was confident she could kill the fuckers. After all, she'd already got one.

"Sorry. I'm just scared, is all."

"Everyone is scared. But at least we're doing something. This is what your great-aunt would have wanted, don't you think?"

"Sure. She struck me as being a tough ol' broad in the true sense of the word. Would have to have been to be one of only two women on that trip, and to have survived as long as she did."

Though Nat wasn't squeamish, the lack of food combined with the sight of her own blood made her feel lightheaded. "I'm going to have to sit down."

"You've earned it. This place looks properly abattoir-like." Droplets, streaks, and smears of her blood decorated the nylon floor and walls of the tent. Nat couldn't smell it, but she was willing to bet she knew something that could. "Should we try our hand at whittling?"

"We shall. Let's go. This place is giving me the creeps."

* * *

The group had an early supper so they'd be finished well before dusk. They avoided calling it a farewell dinner, though everyone understood it most likely was.

Over a meal of lasagna, they toasted each other with tiny cups that held the very last of Igor's moonshine.

"Na zdorovie!" Igor yelled, hoisting his cup in the air. It looked like a thimble in his hand.

"Na zdorovie," the remaining three repeated in unison.

"I'd like to say something, if I might." Nat rose to her feet.

"Speech, speech." Andrew waved his ski pole in the air. How lucky for them that the snowmen had stolen the skis but left the poles. If you could call any part of this adventure lucky.

"In spite of our rocky start, and the many bumps along the road"— she looked at Steven, and the mountaineer raised his glass to her—"I've really enjoyed being out here with you guys. We've made a good team, sometimes in spite of ourselves, and if we continue to work together, I know we will make it out of here alive. I don't just think; I *know*."

The men cheered and hooted. This was one time when they wanted to make as much noise as possible. Let the snowmen come to shut them up. She hoped it would be the last thing those monsters ever tried.

"We cannot show mercy. Remember what they have done to our friends. We are doing this not as heartless killers, but as survivors. To avenge the deaths of Joe, Anubha, Lana, and Vasily. We cannot hesitate. As long as one of them is alive, we are not safe here."

"Don't forget about me. Fuckers busted my leg. If it weren't for them, we'd be halfway down the mountain already," Igor said. The firelight reflected in his blue eyes, making him look otherworldly, like some creature who had ascended from hell to avenge them. Nat wished they had that kind of supernatural power on their side, rather than four hikers armed with ski poles and their wits.

"And Igor's leg! We must seek justice for Igor's leg." Andrew thrust his cup into the air with such zeal she would have thought he was drunk, except for the fact there wasn't enough alcohol left in camp to get a mouse tipsy.

"For Igor's leg," everyone cried.

Soon after, the howling began.

The group now recognized the sound for what it was—a battle cry. The levity they'd enjoyed seconds before vanished.

"I-I'm not sure I can do this," Andrew said, giving voice to what she was sure everyone was thinking. If there were three or four creatures, they might have a chance. But what if there were dozens? Or hundreds?

She took his hand in hers, squeezing it. "Yes, you can."

He squeezed back before helping Steven move Igor into position. The Russian slung an arm around each man for balance, but he already moved pretty well on his own, hopping around on his makeshift crutches. Nat cringed each time she saw him hopping on the snow. All it would take was one false step and down he would go. At this point, a single fall could spell his doom.

Within minutes, the tableau of a critically injured man, abandoned and helpless, was complete. Nat hoped they would fall for it.

"You all set, Igor?"

Andrew had covered the Russian up to his neck with a blanket so only his head was visible. Igor grinned. "Bring. It. On." With his heavily accented English, it reminded her of one of Arnie's memorable lines from the *Terminator* movies.

She and Andrew hunkered down on the other side of their newly decorated tent. This close, the fumes were eye-watering. Steven disappeared into the darkness behind Igor. This was the riskiest part of her plan. If something went wrong, they were too far apart to come to each other's aid.

The chorus of howls died abruptly. Somehow, the silence was more ominous. Then she heard Igor holler a string of English and Russian curses that were doubly impressive under the circumstances.

"How could you leave me to die, you fuckers? You heartless cunts. If I ever get my hands on you, I'll tear your eyes out through your ass."

"Eyes through your ass? Interesting turn of phrase," Andrew whispered.

It was the signal. Igor had seen something.

The snowmen had arrived.

Nat prayed fervently, hoping to hear another cry, this one of pain. Entwining her fingers with Andrew's, she prayed that the sweet, sensitive man beside her would be able to access his inner warrior. That the mountaineer would not betray their fragile truce again.

"He's sniffing at it! He knows something's there."

Seizing Andrew by the jacket, she jerked him out of sight behind the tent, her heart pounding. "Are you crazy? They have way better night vision than we do. It might have seen you."

"It didn't see me, but I don't think this is going to work—"

A scream split the night air, but it wasn't the one she'd been waiting for.

It was Steven.

Forgetting how she'd scolded Andrew a second before, she risked a peek, in time to see Steven charge the creature with a makeshift club held aloft.

"What is he doing? This wasn't our plan."

Startled, the snowman moved back a step, and that was all it took. The ground beneath him gave way and everything but his hooded head disappeared from view. Steven was on him in a second, swinging his club at the creature's face as though it were a baseball. Blood spattered on the snow, but he didn't stop. He swung again and again, until a sickening crunching sound brought an end to the terrible howls and snarls coming from the pit.

The mountaineer tossed his club on the snow, panting. Steam rose from his head into the frosty air, making him look like he was on fire.

"Right on, Steven. I can't believe it worked." Andrew moved to join him, but Nat grabbed his coat again.

"There are more of them. You have to stay here." She crossed her fingers, hoping Steven would recover his strength quickly. There was no time for celebration, not yet, and he was in a vulnerable position, with his back facing the woods.

As if he'd read her mind, the mountaineer scooped up his club and vanished into the shadows behind Igor again. The Russian gave him a thumbs-up as he passed. One down, but how many to go?

She'd never agreed to any of them facing the creatures head on. The monsters were too powerful. Judging by the defensive wounds on Dyatlov and Vladimirovich's hands, the Russian skiers had made that mistake. But in this case, Steven thankfully had had the element of surprise working in his favor. Otherwise, the pit they'd spent hours digging would have been a waste of time.

"Welcome, you ugly bastard. Come to finish me off, have you? Why don't you come over here and suck my dick?"

Igor again. With the pit uncovered, there wasn't much left to protect him.

"Let's see if we can get it to come over this way," Nat whispered. Her lantern flared in the darkness, hopefully making it appear that they were inside the shelter rather than beside it. Holding a dry corner of the tent, she jostled it, forcing herself to laugh like she'd heard the world's funniest joke. "It's going to be great to get home, I tell you. I can't *wait* to sleep in my own bed."

"Me either. After I spend a full day in the hot tub, I'm going straight to Urasawa and ordering everything they have." Andrew's tone matched her wistful joviality perfectly. Only someone who knew him well would have picked up on the fear underneath.

She listened hard for a moment, but heard nothing. "Sounds fantastic. Count me in. We'll make a party out of it."

A long, low howl very different from the ones they'd heard earlier that evening made her jump.

"I think he's found his friend," Andrew said.

The sound ended as abruptly as it had begun. While they waited, the cold from the snow underneath them crept into her bones. She held her breath, listening for anything that would tell her where the creature was.

Scraping and rustling noises came from the direction of the pit.

"Never mind him. Look at me, you fucker. What are you doing, you ugly prick? I was saving that for my dinner, you sad fuck."

Igor's taunts gave her the courage to risk another peek. The snowman had lifted his dead comrade from the pit and slung him over his shoulder. In the firelight, his coat looked oddly shiny, like no hide she'd ever seen. Despite his immense strength, the creature staggered under his buddy's weight, his feet sinking into the snow.

"He's taking him. We can't let him leave."

Andrew raised an eyebrow. "How are we supposed to stop him?"

"I don't know, but we have to do something. Otherwise, we'll be stuck waiting for him again."

Among their homemade arsenal was one true weapon: Anubha's crossbow. There was only one problem: none of them knew how to use it. Nat had been dumb enough to mumble something about archery classes in high school, so the men had entrusted her with the sleek, aluminum contraption that bore no resemblance to the clunky, wooden thing she'd struggled with as a teenager.

Still, if Jennifer Lawrence could manage a bow in *The Hunger Games*, how difficult could it be? After several tries, Nat could only hope she'd managed to load it correctly.

Adrenaline racing through her veins, she leapt to her feet before she could think better of it. Pulling away from Andrew's grasp, she stepped out from the tent into the open. The snowman was past the fire, making his way to the tree line now. A few more steps and he'd be gone. Taking a deep breath, she raised the crossbow, doing her best to sight it.

"Hey! Where do you think you're going?" she yelled.

"Nat, are you insane? He's too far away. Get back here," Andrew said, but she held her ground, and as the monster turned, she fired. With the full force of her fear and rage behind her, the bolt went farther than she'd expected, hitting the creature square in the hood. From the resulting squeal, it had pierced the strange hide and found flesh. Snarling, the snowman tossed his friend to the ground as though the body were a sack of leaves. It came for her, closing the distance between them with frightening speed.

"Nat, run!"

"Stick to the plan," was all she had time to say before she ducked inside the tent, praying with everything she had that the creature would come after her and leave Andrew alone.

A second later, the snowman tore open the front of the tent with its claws. She screamed, the suddenness of its movements more frightening than its dark form charging her. Scrambling backward, she crawled toward the hole the snowman had slashed in the side the night before. Fresh air assaulted her face—her upper body was free. Now to—

Her right leg was pinned, trapped. The creature had hold of her ankle and it was like being wedged in a vise. There was no give, no leeway. She felt hot breath against her skin as her snow pants tore and she cried out, begging for help that wouldn't come in time. This was her plan, this was the way she had wanted it. If she fell, she wouldn't take anyone with her.

But she'd never expected to fall.

"Do it now," she shouted at Andrew, accepting all she was about to sacrifice.

"But you're still inside!"

"I don't care. Do it anyway."

For a second, time stopped. Impossibly, Nat heard the click of Andrew's lighter over the creature's snarling and her own harsh panting.

A fireball engulfed the tent as the creature screeched. The roar of the inferno, the intensity of the heat on her face, was blistering. Something seized her under her arms and ripped her backward. Her boot came free and Nat yelped as her bare foot was pulled through the blaze.

"Jesus Christ. What were you thinking?"

Steven. He didn't let go until they were halfway across the campsite. Her tent, soaked with her own blood as bait and Igor's moonshine as accelerant, burned brightly enough to turn night into day. And still the creature shrieked. Nat pressed her hands over her ears.

"Where's Andrew?" Panic crushed her, making it impossible to breathe.

Then she saw him, over near Igor, his eyes wide enough to swallow his face. Did he get that she'd escaped, or did he believe he'd burned his best friend alive? She yelled to him, but he continued to gape at the tent.

"Don't bother. No one can hear you over that. How's the foot?"

Her foot. Wincing, she surveyed the damage. The right leg of her snow pants was ripped to shreds. Her sock was literally hanging by a thread, and her ski boot was gone. But the foot itself was okay, thanks to Steven. She wiggled her toes and gasped at the resulting sting. Singed, and probably soon to be frostbitten, but she'd gotten off lightly, all things considered.

"Here, put these on." Steven handed her two wool socks from his own pack, and she gratefully pulled them over her bare skin, ignoring the throbbing from the burn. She hadn't seen any blistering, so hopefully she didn't have to worry about an infected foot on top of everything else. Losing the boot was enough of a catastrophe.

"Lana's boots should fit you. We'll go get them as soon as it's light."

She cringed. "I can't do that."

"Nat, she's dead. They're of no use to her anymore. And you can't go without. Not if you want to get home."

It made sense. Why leave perfectly good ski boots to rot when she was in need? But, common sense or not, she couldn't imagine stealing the boots from a dead girl's feet.

Best to change the subject.

"Do you think we got them all?"

Steven squinted at her, as if trying to decide whether or not to tell the truth. "I wish I could say yes, but there were a lot more than two of them making that racket tonight. You know it as well as I do."

Andrew called her name. She looked up to see him waving at her, an expression of ecstatic joy on his face. So he *had* thought he'd killed her.

As he started toward her, something loomed out of the shadows behind him. Intent on their reunion, her friend didn't hear it.

"Andrew, no! Look out!"

But it was too late.

The creature seized him by the neck, lifting him off his feet. There was a moment when his eyes stared into hers with a dreadful knowing.

The snowman twisted Andrew's neck, killing him instantly and tossing him to the ground. His body flopped like a doll's.

Nat sank to her knees, in too much emotional pain to move or cry. *He can't be gone. Not Andrew. I can't survive without Andrew.*

With a roar, Igor sprang upright on his good leg and stabbed the snowman in the face with Joe's knife. He struck the creature again and again, mindless of the gore that gushed from within the hood to splatter his face.

More shadows appeared behind him.

She finally found her voice. "Igor!"

Steven lifted her from the snow, dragging her toward the forest. "We have to go, Nat."

"We can't leave him." She jerked her arm out of his grasp. She tried to run to Igor, but her sock slipped on the ice, giving Steven a chance to take hold of her again.

"Look how many there are. We have to go, *now*. If you want to live, come with me."

~ CHAPTER TWENTY ~

Upon waking, there was a blissful moment of ignorance before the pain of losing Andrew came back to her. Moaning, she pressed her face into the snow, the heat of her tears turning the surface beneath her to ice.

A hand touched her shoulder. "Nat, you'll suffocate. Please don't do that."

The agony was overwhelming, so intense it felt physical, like having a limb ripped from its socket. She *was* missing a limb, would always be. Without Andrew, she had nothing. In so many ways, he'd been the love of her life.

"Leave me alone. Just let me die."

"Sorry, no can do. Andrew would never forgive me if I did, and the last thing I want is his ghost haunting me for the rest of my life. We may not survive, Nat. But don't you think we owe it to them to at least try?"

She pressed her face deeper into the snow. Ice crystals filled her nostrils, and she felt the welcome pressure on her chest as her lungs struggled for air. Fingers grasped her hair close to the roots, wrenching her upright. The freezing air hit her face like a slap.

"Ouch!"

"You have to stop feeling sorry for yourself. We don't have the luxury."

She narrowed her eyes. "Fuck you."

"Maybe later, when our body heat runs low. For now, we have more important things to worry about." Incredibly, he grinned at her. She shuffled forward, kicking his boot with hers.

"How can you *smile* when they're dead? They're all dead." The sob caught in her throat. "They're gone."

"Because we're alive, Nat. And damn lucky to be here, drawing breath. My focus is on survival, not self-pity. Have you forgotten I lost someone too?"

She turned away, sniffling. "That's different. You knew Lana for a few days. I've known Andrew for most of my life."

"Maybe I loved her enough for a lifetime in those few days. Did you ever consider that?"

"I'm sorry." She wiped her face on her sleeve. "I'm finding it hard to care about anyone else's pain right now."

"It's okay; I understand. As much as I can. I've never had someone be as close to me as Andrew obviously was to you. But that's what you have to hold on to. Honor his life, not his death."

"Easy to say; impossible to do."

"I get that. And you have nothing to prove to me, Nat. You've already shown more guts than I ever gave you credit for."

She sniffed, looking past him. "Where are we?"

Her surroundings were white, white, nothing but white. It was like being in an igloo.

"The ravine. I found it yesterday. I was going to tell you, but I never got the chance. We had…other things to discuss." His cheeks reddened.

"The ravine? You mean the same one where—"

"Where my great-aunt died, yes. It's been my mission to find it, though I never thought it would save our lives. It's fitting, in a way. Lyudmila would have liked that."

She swallowed hard and considered the ill-fated young woman. Nat wasn't comfortable living in Lyudmila's tomb, but what choice did she have? "I don't mean to be a pessimist, but have you forgotten what happened to her? I don't think it's safe for us to stay here."

"No, I haven't forgotten. But there has to be a reason she lived longer than the others. All we need is a couple of days, just enough time to rest and give things a chance to calm down. Then we'll leave."

She knew she should thank him for saving her life—for staying calm in a crisis and getting her the hell out of there before she hurtled into her own death. But she couldn't. Not yet. She figured Steven of all people was smart enough to understand. "What if we don't *have* a couple of days?"

"Look, nearest I can tell, Lyudmila's group made some mistake, and that's when the creatures found them. Maybe they thought it was safer to leave the ravine at night; who knows? All we have to do is not make the same mistake they did, and we'll be fine."

"How are we supposed to avoid it, when we don't know what their mistake was?"

He shrugged. "We've been able to observe these things for days. We've witnessed what they sound like, when they move, how they kill. Now we have to use that knowledge to our advantage. We're going to get out of here, Nat. I promise you. You will not die in this ravine."

His words were small comfort. Even less so when she heard a scraping noise and saw he was digging at the roof of their shelter.

"What are you doing?" she hissed at him, kicking the sole of his boot again.

"Making a hole."

"I can see that. But why?"

"So I can get out."

"Are you crazy? They could be standing right outside, waiting." But as her paranoia quickened her pulse, she already knew it wasn't true.

She'd have been able to smell them. The snowmen had their own particular stench, a pungent aroma of dust, body odor, and rotting meat.

"They travel at night, Nat. I assume they sleep during the day."

"That's a big assumption to make. And a dangerous one."

"I prefer to call it an educated guess. Anyway, it has to be done. I need to get you those boots."

"You're *not* leaving me here alone." As awful as it was being stuck with him in the snow cave, the thought of being alone was so much worse.

"And once you have the boots, we'll go together to get supplies."

"We can't go out there. That's what they're waiting for. What if they've taken over our camp? We killed their friends; I'm sure they want to kill us."

"We have to risk it. It's either a quick death out there or a slow death in here. We need supplies, Nat. We won't live long on snow."

By now, he'd dug a hole large enough to expose his head. Putting on his shades, he wiggled his way outside. She bit her lip to keep from crying out, certain something ghastly was going to happen. She kept seeing Andrew's death, over and over again, the anguished expression on her friend's face, until her chest squeezed so tight she could barely get air. The feeling of being buried alive intensified.

Steven lowered his arms, dropping back inside their shelter. "It's clear. I should only be a few minutes."

"Please don't leave me here. I'll go with you." In her panic, she clutched his pant leg. With a bemused smile, he pried off her fingers.

"I can move faster without you. I'll be right back, I promise. You have to start trusting me, Nat."

"This isn't about me not trusting you. It's about me not trusting *them*."

Pulling her toward him, he kissed the top of her head. "I'll be right back. Wish me luck."

And then there were two, she thought as she watched him disappear through the hole he'd dug.

She hoped she wouldn't have to revise that number down to one.

* * *

Nat had expected to go half-mad waiting for him to return, but before she could blink, he was shaking her awake.

"Here, put these on." He thrust Lana's boots into her arms, and her stomach churned at the faint smell of decay. "Quick. We have to hurry. I found Igor."

Perhaps it was the lack of food, or she was groggy from the unexpected nap, but he wasn't making sense. "Why the rush? Is it getting late?" Ensconced in their cocoon of snow, she had no idea of the time.

"You don't understand. I found Igor, and he's *alive*."

She came to life herself, her stiff fingers fumbling with the bootlaces. Igor, alive! When she'd last seen him, he'd been surrounded by the creatures. How on earth had he survived? "How bad is he?"

Steven grimaced. "He's not great. I honestly don't know how much longer he'll live, but we can't leave him there. At least, I can't, but I need your help to bring him here."

"How did you find him? I thought you were going for the boots."

"The coast seemed clear, so I kept going, figured I'd grab some supplies on my own. The more we can get, the better." He gestured to a full pack she hadn't noticed. It was Joe's, so she guessed it contained what was left of their food, not that those dehydrated packets would be much good to them without a fire. Hopefully Steven was right and they'd only be hiding here for a couple of days before descending. The important thing was that they were alive and that they continued to stay that way.

As soon as she'd tied the second boot, Steven was through the hole in the snow and reaching back for her. It was tougher to get out than it looked. As he pulled on her arms and she leaned forward, trying to use her body weight as leverage, she realized how much strength she'd lost. If something happened to Steven, would she be able to leave the ravine, or would she be trapped, helpless, until the snowmen found her?

She emerged into a sparkling wonderland. New snow had fallen during the night, capping the trees in crystalline white.

"Do you still have your sunglasses? Wear them. With this much sun, there's a considerable risk of going snow-blind."

Nat did what he said, not minding his bossiness. In her current state of brain fog, it was a relief to be told what to do.

"Here." He handed her a pair of snowshoes. Anubha's. While she gawked at them like they were some bizarre relic from another era, Steven bent to fasten a pair to his own feet. Joe's fit him well. There would no longer be any question of how to share them among the group, she realized sadly.

"You have been busy."

"I did my best to get everything I thought we could use as quickly as I could." He shot her a worried look, brow furrowing. "We're going to have to pass them...and Lana...on the way back to camp. Can you handle it?"

The thought made her want to melt into the snow and disappear. "I think so."

"My advice? Try not to look. For some reason, Lana…well, she's not in a good way. She's going fast." His voice broke. "Soon she won't be recognizable."

It was cold enough that the bodies should have remained intact until the spring thaw, but she remembered the same thing had happened with some of the Dyatlov victims. Several members of their team had decomposed much faster than the others, in a manner that defied scientific explanation. Another mystery that would forever be unsolved, unless she could figure out what had made Lana's death different from the others'.

They set off through the woods, their footsteps nearly silent on the fresh snow. The shoes made it a lot easier to walk, and Nat was grateful Steven had had the courage and forethought to get them.

She stared at a point between his shoulder blades, figuring it was safest, but every now and then she glanced at the path they were cutting through the forest. It might as well have been a neon sign. "What about our tracks? We'll lead them right to us."

"Don't worry. When we get back, I'll use a cedar branch to get rid of them. That's another reason we have to hurry. We can't risk running out of time."

Nat's stomach growled, but then recoiled as she caught a whiff of rotting meat. Sickly sweet, it made her gorge rise until she was sure she would vomit. "It's them, isn't it?" she asked, not daring to look.

"No, that's Lana. She's even worse than she was earlier this morning. Put your hand on my shoulder and let me guide you. Don't look. Trust me, you don't want to see this."

Breathing through her mouth, she squeezed her eyes shut, gripping Steven's shoulder with all her strength. She forced herself to concentrate on his movements and the sound of his progress, matching him step for step. A sensation akin to vertigo urged her to open her eyes, to take a peek, but she resisted. She didn't need any more fodder for her nightmares.

"Okay, we're past."

She knew without his telling her. The air was clean and crisp again, free from the cloying stench of death.

"What about Andrew?" Nat was hardly able to say his name.

"I've covered him, don't worry. For what it's worth, it doesn't look like he suffered. Can't say that about the rest of us."

She moved close enough to put her hand on his shoulder again. "Thank you." As much as she longed to see her dear friend again, it would completely undo her. Their focus had to be on the living until they got home. Once they were off this terrible mountain there would be time to grieve.

In the harsh light of day, their campsite resembled a war zone. Not much remained of her charred tent but the poles and a few blackened strips of cloth. Gray ash, looking like piles of salt and pepper, littered the ground. In spite of the fresh snow, some of the blood and gore was still visible. Ski poles had been bent and twisted into garish modern-art sculptures. Makeshift clubs and other wood fragments speckled the ground.

But worst of all was Igor.

The Russian moaned when he saw her, and she clapped her hand over her mouth before she could scream. Steven should have warned her.

The skin on the right side of his face was in bloody tatters. His eyelid drooped and his nose had been smashed flat. Someone—no doubt Steven—had covered him with a blanket, so mercifully his body was hidden from view. When she reached him, she collapsed, taking his hands in hers. They were cut and scratched, but were in a much better condition than his face.

"Don't cry," he slurred. "I'm all right."

The obvious lie made her cry harder. If a snowman had appeared in front of her at that moment, she would have killed it with her bare hands. So many good people dead or dying and for what? These creatures killed for the joy of it. There was no other explanation.

"Come on, Nat. We have to go. It's going to take us a while to get him back."

Igor rolled his eyes to Steven's. "Leave me," he said, and she saw most of his teeth were either missing or broken. The pain must have been excruciating.

The mountaineer didn't dignify the Russian's pleas with a response. "I think, between the two of us, we should be able to pull him to the ravine on a sleeping bag. We'll need to move quickly, but the fresh snow will work in our favor."

Nat felt the opposite—that had it been packed, it would have made the journey easier, but there was no point arguing. "Okay," she said, wishing she felt stronger. All she wanted to do was curl into a ball, go to sleep, and escape from this living nightmare. "What do you want me to do?"

"I'll need your help getting him on the bag. After that, we pull. Can you check the tents for the slipperiest bag you can find? I'll pack some more supplies while you look."

The work was a welcome distraction from Igor's condition. Patting his hand and kissing the top of his head, careful to avoid the wound that dissected his skull, she hurried to Lana's tent first. The Olympian had owned the best in high-tech gear; it was the likeliest place to start.

Inside, Nat was struck by the smell of her. Not the sickening decay she'd experienced earlier, but the scent of a healthy, living woman who'd favored jasmine soap. Tears burned her eyes, but she forced them away. *Focus.* She soon saw that her instincts had been good but not great. Lana's bag *was* slippery, but it was also cocoon-style. It didn't fold flat and wouldn't be large enough to hold the Russian.

Holding the tent flap aside, she nearly ran smack into Steven.

"Never mind—turns out Igor's own bag is perfect. We can start rolling him onto it now," he said.

Nat steeled herself for the job ahead. "Is he okay?" she whispered. "I mean, obviously he's not, but is there anything wrong with his body, anything I should know?"

"He's got a nasty wound across his abdomen. Some of his…insides were exposed. I did my best to put them back in the right place, and I packed the opening with some gauze, but once we have him safely in the ravine, he's going to need stitches. And bandages. We might not have enough."

Swallowing hard, Nat ignored the waves of nausea that threatened to overwhelm her. "Okay. Anything else?"

"That's all I could see. His splint is gone, so I wouldn't be surprised if his leg is rebroken, and there might be more nastiness going on internally, but if we get him to a place where we can give him some serious first aid, he might make it."

There were plenty of obstacles: the weather, the fresh snow, the challenge of carrying the Russian's weight all that way, and the creatures, who could be anywhere. But the last thing Nat had expected was for *Igor* to be the most formidable.

"No," he said when he saw them coming with the bag. He shook his head, making his loose flesh wobble and spatter the snow with blood. "No, *nyet.*"

"Come on, Igor. Don't do this. We have to get you out of here."

Nat had never heard Steven sound so kind, so patient. Was this the same man who'd been determined to abandon Andrew?

"No!" Igor's protests echoed through the frigid air, and she cringed, expecting one of those appalling creatures to come charging through the forest at any moment. "Leave me."

She reached for his hand. He was frantic enough that she was worried he'd strike her, but he wrapped his fingers around her palm as if she were a lifeline. "Please, Igor, you have to help. We have to take you with us. We can't just abandon you."

Tears streamed from his good eye. "Leave me. Please. You need to get out of here. You must go. Me, I am already dead."

Nat met Steven's eyes. They couldn't possibly transport the Russian if he wasn't willing to cooperate. He had already suffered too much blood loss, too much shock. The stress of the moving alone could kill him; an out-and-out struggle would do him in.

The mountaineer whistled under his breath. Looking into the distance, he grimaced. "Shit. We're too late. Here they come."

Before she could move, Steven struck. As soon as Igor turned his head to look, the mountaineer got his arms around the man's neck in a chokehold. The Russian's eyes bulged and he clawed at Steven's sleeves. For an agonizing second, Nat thought Igor would break free, but the man's diminished strength worked in their favor. She stifled a cry as the Russian fell backward, unconscious.

"Don't just stand there, help me. We have to hurry. I'm not sure how long he'll stay out."

Moving the unconscious Igor was like grappling with a life-size concrete statue. The two of them grunted and groaned until sweat poured down their faces, but finally they managed to roll the Russian onto his sleeping bag, trying to be as mindful of his wounds as possible.

Mission accomplished, Nat collapsed onto the snow, panting. "Do you really think we're going to be able to get him to the ravine?"

Steven took her by the wrist, tugging her to her feet. "We have no choice. I'm not leaving him here. Once we get some momentum going, we should be fine."

Shouldering one of the team's packs, he handed her another. As she slid it on, she couldn't help but stare at the blanket-covered mound that was Andrew's body.

"I'm sorry," Steven said, touching her arm. "There's no time."

That wasn't Andrew anyway, she told herself. It was only a shell, a shadow of the man she'd loved and would always love. The real Andrew had escaped this place. She hoped he'd landed somewhere good, where the drinks were strong and the men gorgeous.

"Ready?" Steven gave her a corner of Igor's sleeping bag.

Wiping her eyes, she nodded. "As I'll ever be."

"Hey, what's going on? What are you guys doing?" They turned to see the Russian blinking at them, struggling to sit up.

They froze, barely daring to breathe, and then Steven smiled.

"We're going on a little trip, buddy. We'll be there soon. Go back to sleep, okay?"

"Okay." Igor slumped back on the sleeping bag, leaving Nat weak with relief.

Steven's grin vanished. "Let's get moving. If he wakes up again, it might not be so easy."

Gritting her teeth, she put her weight into it, feeling herself falling backward. It was hopeless. The Russian was simply too heavy. The muscles in her arms strained past their limits, but finally the bag began to move.

"Keep pulling," Steven said. "If we stop, it'll be that much harder to get going again."

She didn't bother to respond. Even with the snowshoes, every step she took sank into the fresh powder before taking hold. It required an astonishing amount of energy to put one foot in front of the other. How would she make it to the ravine?

Igor moaned, but thankfully remained unconscious. *Was he sleeping, or had he passed out from the pain?* She couldn't survive another struggle with him or stand to hear his desperate pleas. After an interminable length of time, they at last reached the edge of the clearing. The path to the ravine lay before them, heaped with snow. She felt the urge to weep. There was no way they could carry Igor through this, no way. He was too heavy and they were too depleted.

"Don't stop, Nat. Keep going. We're almost there," Steven lied. "Just look at your feet. Focus on each step, and before you know it, this will be over."

The mountaineer wasn't even out of breath. She would have hated him if she'd had the energy.

Pull, slide. Pull, slide.

After a treacherous moment when it appeared Igor's sleeping bag would slip right off the path, they managed to get it moving again. Fortunately, it was a bit easier than traversing the campsite had been, but it was far from effortless. Nat's breath came in short gasps that burned her lungs. Her hands shook, the sweat coating her fingers making it difficult to maintain her grip on the bag.

Pull, slide. Pull, slide.

"You're doing great. Remember, we can't let them win. We can't. We can't let them take another one of us without a fight."

She wheezed, wondering how Steven had enough wind left in him to be a cheerleader.

His words echoed in her brain, becoming a chant. *We can't let them win. We can't. We can't let them win.*

In all the excitement, if she could call it that, she forgot about Lana until the smell hit. She'd forgotten to avert her eyes.

The woman's face was a swollen, mottled purple. Her hands were clenched as **though** she'd died in the middle of a boxing match, but the skin hung from her bones in shreds. Nat's gorge rose before she could stop it, and she turned her head to the side, vomiting on the snow.

"We can't stop." The urgency in Steven's voice drove her forward. It bordered on shrill. "Don't stop; keep moving."

Breathing through her mouth, Nat drove the grotesque image from her mind. That thing wasn't Lana, like the body at the campsite wasn't Andrew. Their friends were gone, safely away from here.

"That—isn't—her—Steven," she said between gasps.

His eyes narrowed, intent on the path ahead. "I know. Don't think about it. Just keep moving."

So she did. She moved until every muscle in her legs, arms, and back screamed for mercy. She pulled until spots swarmed in front of her eyes and she felt she would faint. Sooner or later, she *would* faint. But until she fell unconscious on the snow, she wouldn't give up. At some point, saving Igor had become everything. Steven's conviction was contagious. She would not leave her friend at the snowmen's mercy. He belonged with her.

She hoped he'd live long enough to see the ravine.

"Well done."

Weary, half snow-blind in spite of her sunglasses, Nat lifted her weary eyes to Steven. He raised an arm to hold her back, to halt her momentum. "You can stop pulling now. We're here."

She gaped at the snow-covered valley before them. She would have never noticed it on her own, and if Steven hadn't stopped her, she would have pulled Igor right off the ledge.

Nat had to hand it to him. It was one hell of a good hiding place.

"I'll lower you down first. I'm going to need your help with Igor. You'll have to catch his legs. Do you think you can do that?"

"I hope so." She felt limper than a used dryer sheet. She had nothing left, and yet she knew that's when humans often showed the greatest resources of strength. Nat hoped she'd be one of them.

Steven gestured to the hole he'd dug. In the glare of the still-bright sun, it wasn't easy to find. Lowering herself to the ground, Nat resisted the urge to sleep, but instead wiggled backward until her feet dangled over the opening. Taking hold of her hands, the mountaineer lowered her into the ravine. She staggered when her feet hit the ground but managed to regain her balance before she fell. Scanning the cave for enemies, she sighed with relief when she saw their packs, and only their packs. What if the snowmen had been inside, waiting for them? It was a horrible thought.

"You ready?"

She wasn't, but she agreed. What else could she do? They hadn't come that far to leave the Russian outside.

The circle of blue in the ceiling was blotted out by the black tread of a large ski boot. Nat caught a glimpse of Steven's gloves as he shoved Igor's other foot through the crack. Snow drifted down to frost her hair and face. She started when the coldness hit her neck, melting as it made contact with her bare skin.

"Hold him around the calves, but be careful of the break. If he gets a good jolt of pain it could wake him up, and this would *not* be a good time for that."

Wrapping her arms around his legs, Nat held on with all her remaining strength, cautious of not applying pressure in the wrong place.

"Okay, I'm going to lower him down. See if you can guide him into a prone position away from the entrance."

Igor's weight was immense, but she was surprised to find she could support him. Before long, she was holding the Russian's hips, and she could see Steven's hands gripping Igor under the armpits.

How on earth is he managing this? Just how strong was he?

"You can let his good foot touch the ground to take some of the weight off, but not the bad one. Be careful."

Straining, she struggled under the Russian's mass, with the absurd image of dancing with a gigantic doll running through her head. She kept her footing for a moment, but then Igor's unconscious form fell forward, crushing her underneath him and forcing the air from her lungs.

Steven was there in a flash, rolling the big man off her. "Are you all right?"

She had to take several deep breaths before she could answer. "I think so. He just knocked the wind out of me."

"It's getting late. The sun will set soon. I need to get rid of our tracks." Steven cast a wary glance at the opening, and Nat noticed the shadows had grown longer.

The idea of being left alone with Igor didn't thrill her, but it was a necessary evil. The tracks were a beacon announcing their location.

"Can you see to him while I'm gone?"

The Russian's breathing was frighteningly loud in the enclosed space. "How do you mean?"

"You know, change his bandages, set up a bed of sorts, make sure he's comfortable. Best to do everything while he's unconscious so he won't feel the pain."

Her stomach writhed, turning anxious somersaults. Now she was going to have to deal with something that would give a military medic pause. "Maybe *I* should get rid of the tracks. I don't really know much about the first aid stuff."

"You know as much as I do. I've been making it up as I go along. Do the best you can, and be gentle."

"Wait." She grabbed his arm before he could pull himself through into the outside world. "Why can't I be the one who goes, and you stay here?"

"Because there's always a chance whoever leaves won't come back. And I'd rather that be me."

~ CHAPTER TWENTY-ONE ~

They shared a cold dinner that night, splitting the contents of one of Joe's last foil packets. Dehydrated food wasn't so bad served cold. It was kind of like jerky. Crunchy jerky. By that time, Nat was so hungry she would have eaten almost anything. The wonderful meal they'd enjoyed in Vizhai had taken place a lifetime ago.

Igor slept fitfully, his breath coming in painful-sounding snorts through his broken nose. They'd been unable to rouse him or get him to eat. Now that his face was clean and bandaged, it was easier to look at him without wincing, but any help she'd been able to give him was mostly cosmetic. For the Russian to survive, emergency medical treatment would be essential.

"What if he doesn't wake up?"

Moistening his finger, Steven poked it into the corner of the foil packet to pull out the last bit of seasoning. "Honestly, it's probably better for him if he doesn't. I can't imagine how much pain he's in. It must be unbearable."

"What about all the blood? Won't it lead them right to us?" The thought had been nagging at the edges of her brain. She had no proof that blood was a lure—only her instincts had made her spill her own around her tent. But, assuming the creatures were more animal than human, it was a safe bet.

The mountaineer shrugged, never taking his attention away from the foil packet. His obvious hunger was a reminder of the desperateness of their situation. They were running low on food, and with Igor in his current state, there would be no leaving Dead Mountain. At some point in the not-too-distant future, impossible choices would have to be made. "It might."

His nonchalance angered rather than comforted her. "Doesn't that worry you?"

"I don't see much point in worrying. We had no choice. We couldn't leave him there, so we'll have to take our chances. Right?" He cocked an eyebrow at her, daring her to speak the vile truth—that it would have been smarter to have left Igor where he was.

But she refused to be the bad guy. And what if, on some level of consciousness, Igor could hear her? "Right."

As the sun lowered, so had their voices, until they were whispering in the near darkness. "We'll have to leave soon if we want to survive. We can't stay here."

"I know," he said, and the silence stretched out between them. Had they caused Igor further pain and injury, only to abandon him in a day or two? "Maybe one of us should stay behind and look after him while the other goes for help."

"Absolutely not. No way."

"It might be our only chance, Nat."

"I don't care. Whenever one of us has tried to go it alone, they've died. You know what the definition of insanity is. Either we live together or we die together. We are *not* splitting up."

"We can't leave him by himself. Not like this."

We might have to. It was the one thing she could never bring herself to say.

"Besides, the snowmen are nocturnal. All we'd have to do is make good headway during daylight hours. I could be out of their territory by the first day."

"What makes you so certain? We don't know where their territory *is*, where it begins and ends. We don't even know for sure they're nocturnal. Maybe some of them are out and about during the day, and what then? We don't know anything about what they are."

Whenever she'd read stories about yeti sightings, she'd pictured great furry creatures with masses of white hair, certainly not these repulsive things with their glowing yellow eyes and razor-like teeth. Were they a link on the evolutionary chain that Darwin had missed? A bizarre hybrid of some sort that had evolved to live in these mountains?

"The Cold War."

Steven broke into her thoughts, making her jump.

"What?"

"The Cold War. Whatever those creatures are, I bet they have something to do with that. Maybe the Russians tried to make super soldiers, and instead they ended up with——"

"Monsters."

"Yeah."

Nat considered everything she'd seen. Assuming they didn't have a personal shopper, the snowmen were intelligent enough to fashion their own clothes out of hide. They'd shown considerable smarts when it came to killing as well. Igor's survival was nothing short of a miracle, while she and Steven had only dumb luck to thank. Well, dumb luck and the mountaineer's foresight in finding the ravine.

"You really think those things were once human?" she asked.

"I think any humanity was bred out of them a long time ago."

She trembled, remembering the coldness of those ugly, pupil-less eyes. There had been no compassion, no remorse, no hesitancy in them, only cold-blooded murder. Then again, she wondered what other creatures saw in the eyes of her own species. Man wasn't exactly known for his merciful, live-and-let-live nature either. What if the snowmen had been created to embody the worst traits of humanity with none of the good?

"I always thought that yetis, if they existed, would have evolved from the common ancestor we share with apes," she said.

"I'm not sure if they're yetis or not, but there's no way those things are related to apes."

Nat wondered how he could be so sure. They walked upright like humans and had opposable thumbs and fingers like both species. They were obviously capable of using tools, of planning, and of conscious thought. Aside from a few examples found in politics, people looked nothing like their hairy cousins, despite the similarities in DNA. So who was to say the snowmen hadn't simply evolved in a different direction? The eyes and fangs could be modifications selected over time in order to survive such a harsh climate.

"Do you think—" She hesitated, uncertain how to phrase her question. In spite of the forty years that had passed, she could tell it was a sensitive subject. "Do you think this is what happened to your aunt?"

"Yes, I do. What else could it be? Our people have the exact same injuries as her friends."

It was true, but there was so much that couldn't be explained. The radiation on some of the Dyatlov group, the crushing internal injuries, the mysterious burns. Nat's brain spun in circles until she felt dizzy.

"We're not going to solve anything tonight, and the quieter we are, the better, so let's try to get some sleep. Maybe things will be clearer in the morning," Steven said.

In spite of her exhaustion, she couldn't imagine being able to rest. The closeness of the snow around her gave her the feeling of being buried alive. Her chest was so tight it was difficult to breathe. Still, she shuffle-crawled over to Igor. They'd agreed to spend the night in a huddle to conserve body heat, keeping the unconscious Russian warm, though whenever she touched his skin that was less of a concern. The man was burning up.

Refusing to let her mind wander into darkness as she worried about the infection Igor must be fighting, she buried herself in the blankets and cuddled close to the unconscious man, praying he'd be alive in the morning.

The snow crunched underneath Steven as the mountaineer moved to Igor's other side. "Christ," he whispered. "He feels like he's on fire. That's not go—"

The roof caved in, smothering her in cold and darkness. Choking, frantic to free herself, she pawed at the snow that covered her face, hands hooked into claws. Over the pounding of her pulse, she could hear Steven screaming.

Shut up. You'll call them. You'll lead them right to us.

Then she could hear something else, a familiar snarling that made goose bumps spread along her spine. Her bladder clenched in terror. It wasn't a cave-in.

The snowmen had found them.

"Steven!"

He was still screaming, which was awful, but at least it meant he was alive. Her fingers dug through the snow, searching for the knife she'd last seen lying on Steven's sleeping bag. But all too soon the screaming stopped, replaced by a sound a million times more dreadful.

Chewing.

Her hand closed around the hilt of Joe's knife. Digging through the snow, she gouged great chunks of it away from her face, moving blindly toward the appalling sounds. Touching something, she flinched before recognizing the feel of slick fabric—ski pants. Steven's leg, dangling in midair. Reaching upward, she followed the form of his body until she could estimate where the creature was, its guttural growls chilling her blood.

She swung the knife in a wide arc, connecting with something yielding and malleable. Rewarded with an ear-splitting shriek, she thrust the blade forward again and again, hitting her target each time with all her strength. Nat closed her eyes as steaming gore gushed over her face. Her sight was useless anyway. After another anguished, inhuman cry, she heard a soft thump and Steven's body fell against her, knocking her off her feet. She tumbled to the ground, snow cushioning her fall, and dragged the mountaineer away from the cave-in by his jacket.

Gasping, she fumbled for the lantern. Steven would have berated her, told her it wasn't safe, yelled about the glow of the light revealing their location through the snow. She didn't care. The worst had already happened; their location was already compromised. She had to see what she was dealing with.

Steven's lovely blue eyes—the eyes a multitude of women had no doubt swooned over—were fixed on the roof. His mouth was twisted in a grimace. She wept to see the atrocious wound on his neck. Most of the protective flesh was gone, leaving a bloody mess behind. Tying her scarf around the gaping cut, she watched the fabric immediately become saturated with his blood. Laying her head on his chest, her body shaking with sobs, she listened frantically for a heartbeat, though she already knew the truth.

He was gone.

She'd been too late.

"I'll fucking kill you! I will fucking *kill* you, all of you."

"Nat?" A cautious voice spoke in the shadows of the snow cave, making her flinch. It was like hearing a ghost speak. "What's wrong? What happened?"

She raised the lantern. It might as well have been a ghost. Wincing in the glare, Igor lifted a hand to block his good eye. He held his other arm across his abdomen. Incredibly, he'd managed to extricate himself from both his sleeping bag and the cave-in. For a moment, she gaped at him, unable to speak. He should have been dead. The Russian had so many critical injuries it would have been easier to list the parts of him that weren't wounded. And yet he was still alive, still drawing breath, while Steven was...

Nat pointed at the mountaineer's body, crying.

"Oh no! No." Igor shuffled closer, never taking his eyes from Steven's face.

"He's gone." The last word ended in a wail. For all the trouble he had caused, Steven had been their best chance of getting out of there alive. Without his help and guidance, they didn't have a hope in hell.

The enormity of the loss threatened to crush her, and the tears rushed from her in a torrent. Andrew, Lana, Joe and Anubha, Vasily, and now Steven. Igor put his arm around her shoulders, pulling her close. The sound of her grief might bring the creatures back, but once set free it was impossible to stop. Nat sobbed until she had nothing left.

"I thought he would be the one to make it," Igor said. He'd shut off the lantern, but she could feel the presence of the mountaineer's body. In so many ways, Steven had been larger than life. Already she missed his marching orders, his analysis of every situation.

"I thought it would be you." They both acknowledged, without her having to say it, that this wasn't a possibility. The Russian was alive, which was nothing short of a miracle, but it was obvious he was dying. Without sophisticated medical care and a means of leaving the mountain, there was no chance of saving him.

"Looks like it's going to be you. As soon as the sun's up, you have to leave."

"I can't walk out on you, Igor. I won't. Not going to happen." Now that Steven was gone, she was no longer willing to leave the ailing Russian behind. She kept thinking, what if it were her? What if she'd been the one with fatal wounds who had to watch the others abandon her to her fate? What if there were no choice but to lie in this snowy grave, waiting for the creatures to return and tear her apart? The thought made new tears start.

"Listen to me. If you don't get out of here, they will kill you too, and then all of this will have been for nothing. No one will understand what happened to us. We'll become another Dead Mountain mystery like Dyatlov. Steven deserves better than that. Lana deserves better. *Andrew* deserves better. Don't you want him to have a proper burial?"

He took her hand in his, entwining their fingers. Normally, she'd have shied away from such prolonged intimate contact with anyone except Andrew, but the comfort of Igor's touch was welcome, even necessary. The warmth of his hand through their gloves kept her tethered to reality. "I know you're right, but I won't leave you. I can't."

"You have Joe's knife?"

"Yes." She'd somehow managed to keep it with her during her stabbing frenzy and afterward. Its weight in her lap was the only security she had.

"Use it to slit my throat. Wait a minute before you argue. You'd be doing me a favor, Nat. It feels like my whole body is screaming, all the time. It never shuts up. I can't sleep, can't get any peace. I'm in so much pain, but I'll be damned if I let those bastards take me. I want to choose my own death, and I want you to help me. I'll show you where to cut."

She shook her head. "No...no. I can't do that."

"Sure you can. You've killed two of those things now. I'm not going to fight back."

"I can't kill you, Igor. I—I love you." She was surprised to find it was true. At some point, their little group had become her family. It was what she had left to live for. It wasn't worth surviving if she was the only one left.

He squeezed her hand. "I love you too. That's why I'm asking you to do this. I trust you."

"There has to be another way. There *has* to be." Could she get help before Igor succumbed to his injuries or the snowmen returned to finish him off? She wished she'd entertained Steven's idea of splitting up. If she'd let him leave, the mountaineer would be halfway down Kholat Syakhl by now. He'd be alive.

As her adrenaline wore off, her lids grew heavier and heavier, until they felt weighed down with sand. She rested her head on Igor's shoulder, taking comfort in the rise and fall of his massive chest. Nat knew she was drifting, but it felt impossible to stop, like she was a late-night driver hypnotized by the road. Her chin fell to her chest, and she slept.

* * *

A strange scraping sound made her open her eyes. The first thing she saw was Igor's face looming above her. Somehow, she'd ended up with her head in his lap, but before she could register any embarrassment, he held a finger to his lips.

Tilting his head, he indicated something in front of her. Warily, she rolled to the side, moving off Igor's lap and onto her elbows. Weak light filtered into the cave from the ruined section of the roof, and she started to see the prone figure of Steven was moving. *Drag, pause. Drag, pause.* The weird scraping was his body being towed along the snow.

Something was in here with them. Something alien, something evil. She could make out a great, hulking shadow, its claws piercing Steven's hood. Mercifully, the mountaineer's eyes were closed now. She couldn't have handled it if he were staring at her.

When she'd moved off Igor's lap, she'd felt the weight of Joe's knife slide off her legs onto the snow. She felt for the weapon now, but the Russian pressed her arm. "Let it go," he whispered. The creature stealing Steven's body didn't react, though it must have heard. The space was too enclosed for it not to have.

"They can't have him." Her fingers tightened around the knife's hilt, and as if it could read her mind, the creature fixed its hateful yellow eyes on her. She caught a glint of light reflected from its teeth.

"Nat…" Igor urged her close, so he could whisper his next words into her ear. "You don't have the benefit of surprise this time. If you try to stop that thing, it will kill you, and Steven would never want you to die for this. He's dead, Nat. That's just his body. His soul is long gone from this place."

She realized this, accepted it even though she could feel the mountaineer's presence watching over them still. "They can't have him."

"It's not him—it's a body. A corpse. That's all."

"Why can't they leave us alone?" Rage made her body surge with renewed energy, but whenever she tried to move, to grab Steven's leg and pull him back, Igor stopped her.

The creature kept its baleful eyes on her, staring backward as it hauled their friend toward the entrance.

"I imagine they want his skin."

"What?" Her brain refused to process the Russian's words, the image too repulsive to contemplate.

"Its coat—what did you think it was made of?"

The suggestion drove her gaze upward before she could think better of it, away from their dead friend and onto the creature itself and the oddly shiny-looking hide that covered it. The hide had always repulsed her, though she'd never asked herself why. Everything about the creatures had been repulsive. But now she knew. Her stomach filled with ice. Intermingled with the patches of animal fur on its coat were large swatches of human skin.

Something inside her snapped. Those *things* were not going to use any of her friends—her *family*—as their fucking clothing.

Before Igor could react, she dove for the creature, who gaped at her, startled. The shallowness of the cave worked in her favor, as the snowman was hunched over, nearly frog-walking away with its prize. Using both hands, she swung the knife home, plunging it into the thing's eye.

This time, neither the gush of gore nor the metallic-sounding shrieks fazed her. She stabbed again and again, never pausing, her rage and fear driving her to destroy.

"Nat. Nat!"

Whirling around, she saw it was Igor who was trying to restrain her. For a second, she didn't care. She wanted to keep stabbing, keep destroying. The realization horrified her, and the knife fell from her fingers. The sight of the thing at her feet made her gut churn.

The creature's face had been obliterated. Her clothing, the snow, and the snowman's coat were covered in blood and bright yellow fluid. Stumbling away, she vomited until nothing was left but dry heaves.

"You shouldn't have done it," Igor said once she'd rejoined him. "There are more, and they'll come after him. We can't win. There are so many of them and only two of us."

She shuffled forward to retrieve Joe's knife. Settling with her back against the wall of the cave, she focused on the hole in the roof.

"Let them come," she said. "Let them come."

~ CHAPTER TWENTY-TWO ~

Hours passed, but she never faltered.

Eyes narrowed, she stared at the slice of sky visible from the hole in the snow cave's ceiling, waiting.

Steven was on one side of her, Igor on the other. Sometimes she forgot who was dead and who was alive, her only reminder the Russian's ragged breathing.

It didn't matter, in any case. Both were too far gone to help her, like Anubha and Andrew and all the others. She was the hunter now.

She was Death.

Clutching Joe's blade in two hands, she pointed it at the opening and waited. She could be patient. She knew they would come, and when they did, they would die.

The moment before it happened, part of her—the part that was still sane—wondered how it had all gone so terribly wrong. She cuddled closer to Steven, though her friend's body had long grown cold and stiff.

She tensed her muscles as she heard a crunching sound from above. At last, her waiting was over.

She was ready.

A shadow fell across the floor of the cave.

She burst through the roof, blinded by snow, thrusting the knife upward with all her strength.

Her target fell to the ground with a yelp of pain. An all-too-human sound.

"Nyet, nyet! *STOP.*"

A cacophony of shouting. Cruel men's voices surrounded her, followed by an ominous click.

Nat blinked, feeling her fragile sanity return. She lay half in and half out of the ravine, her victim facedown in front of her. Crimson pooled around the wound in his throat where she'd buried Joe's hunting knife. A cry of anguish erupted from her as she recognized the diminutive figure.

Vasily.

As she screamed her rage to the darkening sky, another threatening click came from the circle of men who pressed closer, rifles pointed at her head.

The Russian police.

They stared at her in horror.

What did they see when they looked at her, she wondered. A victim? A survivor? A monster?

Not daring to move, she waited for them to fire.

THE END

ACKNOWLEDGMENTS

I'm eternally grateful to everyone who continues to support these wild stories of mine, especially Hunter Shea, LaVona Parker, Tara Clark, Louise Gibson, Dana Krawchuk and John Toews from McNally Robinson Booksellers, R.J. Crowther Jr. from Mysterious Galaxy Bookstore, Wai Chan, Nikki Burch, and the Insecure Writer's Support Group.

I would never have survived my trek through the Ural Mountains without my personal cheerleaders Simon Fuller and Christine Brandt. Thanks to my copy editor Chris Brogden for his patience and eye for detail.

To all my readers, blog followers, librarians, friends, and family: I couldn't do this without you. Thank you so much for your encouragement and support.

Once again, Gary and the folks at Severed Press have been great to work with, and I'm thrilled to be one of their authors.

CHECK OUT OTHER GREAT HORROR NOVELS

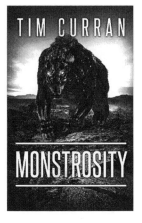

MONSTROSITY
by Tim Curran

The Food. It seeped from the ground, a living, gushing, teratogenic nightmare. It contaminated anything that ate it, causing nature to run wild with horrible mutations, creating massive monstrosities that roam the land destroying towns and cities, feeding on livestock and human beings and one another. Now Frank Bowman, an ordinary farmer with no military skills, must get his children to safety. And that will mean a trip through the contaminated zone of monsters, madmen, and The Food itself. Only a fool would attempt it. Or a man with a mission.

THE SQUIRMING
by Jack Hamlyn

You are their hosts

You are their food.

The parasites came out of nowhere, squirming horrors that enslaved the human race. They turned the population into mindless pack animals, psychotic cannibalistic hordes whose only purpose was to feed them.

Now with the human race teetering at the edge of extinction, extermination teams are fighting back, killing off the parasites and their voracious hosts. Taking them out one by one in violent, bloody encounters.

The future of mankind is at stake.

And time is running out

CHECK OUT OTHER GREAT HORROR NOVELS

BLACK FRIDAY
by Michael Hodges

Jared the kleptomaniac, Chike the unemployed IT guy, Patricia the shopaholic, and Jeff the meth dealer are trapped inside a Chicago supermall on Black Friday. Bridgefield Mall empties during a fire alarm, and most of the shoppers drive off into a strange mist surrounding the mall parking lot. They never return. Chike and his group try calling friends and family, but their smart phones won't work, not even Twitter. As the mist creeps closer, the mall lights flicker and surge. Bulbs shatter and spray glass into the air. Unsettling noises are heard from within the mist, as the meth dealer becomes unhinged and hunts the group within the mall. Cornered by the mist, and hunted from within, Chike and the survivors must fight for their lives while solving the mystery of what happened to Bridgefield Mall. Sometimes, a good sale just isn't worth it.

GRIMWEAVE
by Tim Curran

In the deepest, darkest jungles of Indochina, an ancient evil is waiting in a forgotten, primeval valley. It is patient, monstrous, and bloodthirsty. Perfectly adapted to its hot, steaming environment, it strikes silent and stealthy, it chosen prey: human. Now Michael Spiers, a Marine sniper, the only survivor of a previous encounter with the beast, is going after it again. Against his better judgement, he is made part of a Marine Force Recon team that will hunt it down and destroy it.

The hunters are about to become the hunted.

CHECK OUT OTHER GREAT HORROR NOVELS

DEATH CRAWLERS
by Gerry Griffiths

Worldwide, there are thought to be 8,000 species of centipede, of which, only 3,000 have been scientifically recorded. The venom of Scolopendra gigantea—the largest of the arthropod genus found in the Amazon rainforest—is so potent that it is fatal to small animals and toxic to humans. But when a cargo plane departs the Amazon region and crashes inside a national park in the United States, much larger and deadlier creatures escape the wreckage to roam wild, reproducing at an astounding rate. Entomologist, Frank Travis solicits small town sheriff Wanda Rafferty's help and together they investigate the crash site. But as a rash of gruesome deaths befalls the townsfolk of Prospect, Frank and Wanda will soon discover how vicious and cunning these new breed of predators can be. Meanwhile, Jake and Nora Carver, and another backpacking couple, are venturing up into the mountainous terrain of the park. If only they knew their fun-filled weekend is about to become a living nightmare.

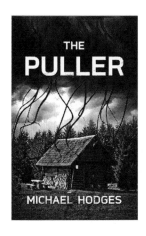

THE PULLER
by Michael Hodges

Matt Kearns has two choices: fight or hide. The creature in the orchard took the rest. Three days ago, he arrived at his favorite place in the world, a remote shack in Michigan's Upper Peninsula. The plan was to mourn his father's death and figure out his life. Now he's fighting for it. An invisible creature has him trapped. Every time Matt tries to flee, he's dragged backwards by an unseen force. Alone and with no hope of rescue, Matt must escape the Puller's reach. But how do you free yourself from something you cannot see?

Made in the USA
Monee, IL
06 March 2020